Halfway to Impossible

by

M.R. Koch

REaDLips Press

Managing Editors: Della Rey & Jack Odman.

Cover Art: R. Bilcliff

For BBK

Table of Contents

2012

They were arranged in a circle, sequestered like a jury in a room with sallow walls that resembled tepid chicken broth. Each Wednesday they met like this and week by week the walls grew tighter. Max tested the temperature of his coffee again and felt only a dull sting on the tip of his tongue where he had been previously scalded. Good enough. He gulped, twice in quick succession, not knowing when Yuri would waddle in with his fuzzy, caramel voice and lead introductions. Tonight was off to a raucous start because Muhammed had brought donuts. He did it as a gag—prompted by a joke that inevitably came up each session about mimicking AA meetings. This wasn't Alcoholics Anonymous, but it was close enough.

Max cringed wordlessly through group meetings, speaking only during the bumpy introductions and when Yuri needed a tonal shift away from the coke and meth-head stories. All in all, it wasn't a bad time—

better than the lobby with its laminated chart of drinks per week, stratified by gender, and the unexplainably cozy futon where one was always pressed up against a twitchy leg or, worse, a shaky hand. The lobby sported one faux fern that stood mockingly high atop the checkerboard porcelain mosaic tiles, undulating falsely whenever the bathroom door flew open and an outstretched arm held a piss cup. The lobby wasn't exactly *unwelcoming* but existed more as a stern reminder when that gray elevator mouth closed that you had not checked into Cliffside Malibu.

"Oh, you haaf donut. OK, OK, that's fine but while you eat let us begin with introductions and, once again, for the new faces please state your drug of choice." Yuri was wearing pleated khakis and a white shirt with vertical red and blue stripes that made him look like a Fourth of July mannequin. He was only a little pudgy and even that was confined to a modest lump above his belt, which made Max wince to think of what tragedy befell him back in Russia to cause that waddling gait.

As he did every week, Marcus kicked things off: "Well as most of you know, I'm Marcus, and I got in trouble with liquor and you know, sometimes I'd be sipping on that purple. Been here damn near six months now, sober pretty much all that time, and this last weekend we had a big sweet 16 party for my daughter at Times Square with limos and everyone." He paused here for Yuri to direct the pattering of applause. "You know, straight up, if this had been one year ago, don't know that I'd a been there. I'm ashamed to say that I missed her last two birthdays. Just went out with the boys and planned to come back in the evening and woke up somewhere else on a different day. She don't quite trust me yet but it was a big step to building back that father-daughter relationship." Max suspected that if Marcus stayed alive long enough, he would one day have Yuri's job. The problem was that Marcus was already over 300 pounds and growing—not to mention that he considered the Jim Beam commercials with Mila Kunis to be a constant threat to his sobriety, as he reminded the others each session.

"Ed, marijuana."

"Javier, marijuana—and some other stuff. Mostly marijuana."

"Mike, cocaine. Marcus, man, thanks for sharing. You guys, that reminds me so much of what happened to me last month, which we talked about, but it reminded me of another story . . . "

"Hey, Mike, we all would laaf to hear your story, but we should perheps first allow everyone to introduce themselves." Yuri was used to this delicate dance with Mike and the other man politely conceded.

"Travis, meth."

"Angie, cocaine." She was the only woman, and despite her squirmy torso and tightly clenched arms she gave Max every indication that she relished the status this afforded her.

"DeShon, liquor."

"Bill, pills." Max suppressed a smile. Hell, he thought, the dude even recites it with an even cadence—downbeat, rest, downbeat, rest. Laughter hardly seemed out of line here, yet Yuri frowned on any silliness during the introductions, so Max bit off the impulse by concentrating on the fire-engine red exit bar that stood inert before the pale door in the corner that surely led to a concrete stairwell.

"Muhammed, uppers."

"Nelson, a little bit of everything, but mostly methamphetamines."

"Max, alcohol." His voice was brassy like a dinged-up coronet and his words felt small.

"Thanks, everyone." Yuri's eyes followed the powder dripping from Mike's jelly donut to the level loop navy carpet. "Tonight I'd like for each of you to think about your support system either waiting for you at home or, well, somewhere out there in the world, perheps a phone call away. Reflect for a moment or two about all the ways they help you out in your day-to-day life and then think about how your actions impact them. What sacrifices have those close to you made on your behef?"

Marcus willed his flabby arm upward, which was merely a token gesture since he was already speaking. "For the first time in years I looked at my daughter with sober eyes on her birthday, and I thought to myself, 'shit, man, this is what I've been missing. I can't fuck this up this time. I got one last shot.' Pardon my language—I know there's a lady in the room. See, when her mom took her from me I didn't know—I had no clue back then how my actions were scaring my family. I just thought, 'OK, if I come home from working all night drivin' that forklift and want to sip on some liquor for a couple hours until my boys come on over to the stoop with a few bottles, then that's my business as a man.' I didn't know—correction, it never even *occurred* to me that my daughter was scared of me when I'd get like that and—"

"Marcus, I hear you," interrupted Mike, who had been nodding along first in solidarity and then as a sort of nervous tick while the anecdote progressed. "My wife had warned me. She said, 'Michael, you smashed up your car and we can't afford for that to happen to mine too. And when she said that, I got so angry that I punched a hole in the wall—right next to her face. Snatched her keys from her purse and split. Stopped at the ATM and withdrew the last $200 from our account with no idea of how we were going to pay rent—nothing—couldn't even think about that. Met my guy, my dealer, and spent every cent we had."

Yuri loved the more cautionary tales, but Mike had been reciting the same story, in competing versions, for weeks. "Thank you, Marcus and Mike, but let's now hear from someone else." He scanned the room. Max stared down at his Starbuck's cup and then locked eyes again with that exit bar. Would it make a screeching noise like a bald eagle or something more akin to those pulsing gestapo sirens in World War II movies? "How about you, Muhammed? Would you like to share with the rest of us?"

"Um, yes. I was driver, and after DWI I lose license so I can no longer work. Out of work three months now and that make me want pills even more than before. But I have good news. My daughter, she is helping me set up new business. We open store soon selling t-shirts with American flags and Statue of Liberty and Twin Towers—stuff like that. Patriotic store. Oh, and we finally have name! We are going to call it American Eagle." Muhammed had a black paint brush mustache and looked like a fit Saddam Hussein.

"I think that name's already taken," said Angie.

"No, it is not."

* * *

From Sheepshead Bay Max took the Q train to Atlantic Center, then walked to the G that took him home—exactly one hour every time. He would try to beat it, shave off a minute or two walking to catch an earlier train, but it was always the same. Once, after a group session, when he was running late for a writers' meeting with his partner, Portia, he paid over $50 for a cab and still, one hour. Since he couldn't seem to improve his routine, he embraced it—*grande* coffee from Starbuck's before and fizzy mineral water from a bodega after, each along the natural side of the road that led away from and back to the train station. Although he knew better, he liked to imagine the trace amounts of lithium in the Gerolsteiner as gifting him some sort of cheap high.

Caroline lay on the couch with her back to him when he entered. The TV played the local news on NY1, but her eyes were closed and she was buried under a purple fleece throw, the corner of her lips parted enough to allow a drop of spit to seep out.

"How was your meeting?" In five years of marriage he had never mastered the art of opening and closing doors without waking her.

"It was fine. Muhammed brought donuts and the fat black guy was in rare form tonight. Cracked me up a few times. How about you? How was work?"

"Awful." She sat up and turned around to face him. "Do you have any idea how shitty it feels to be cussed out by old people all day?" With her makeup already scrubbed off, her face was bloodless, which accented the bluish veins around her eyes. Blond strands clung to one half of her face but jutted wildly, suspended eerily by static electricity, around the other side.

"Sorry. How are you feeling? If you're hungry we should order something."

"I don't want anything to eat."

"You never do." Max moved over next to her on the couch and, brushing some hair from her shoulders, began to massage the scant flesh between her knobby shoulder blades. "You really need to eat more often, Caroline. This is why you never have any energy, I think."

"I hate that I'm stuck doing such a soul-crushing, thankless job, and nobody gets that. Why did we move here? I could have been a God damn social worker in Louisiana or—really anywhere."

"Do I really need to explain it to you again? I have to be here for work, for the type of free-lance assignments I do. This is the only city in America where I—"

"But you don't make any money, sweetie." She turned to face him and he stood and arrowed up the volume on the remote. The weather radar showed a hurricane battering the Caribbean and heading north up the Atlantic as a tropical storm. Jamaica had already been pounded, as footage followed scampering Kingston locals huddling beneath improvised blockades. Impaled by long rusty nails, the boarded windows appeared sturdier than the chipped concrete blocks surrounding them that seemed glued together from assorted broken pieces. At least it's not New Orleans, Max thought, though he didn't dare say the words. "I make some money." Abruptly he turned off the TV. "Come on, I'm going to order Indian with my non-existent money."

"I'm sorry, I'm not trying to be a bitch, but it's true." She reached a hand toward the back of his neck and slowly stroked his skin with her fingernails. He paused momentarily, accepting the gesture as a tomcat does a petting by an erratic child. How did her poor narrow fingers stay so cold even after being bundled up in a blanket? Caroline was always shivering in New York. Even indoors she was rarely without some cocoon—draped in a comforter, layered up in thermals, buried within one of Max's sweaters. Deprived of a southern diet, she had long since sloughed off the patches of baby fat that had irked her throughout her adolescence. But there was a tradeoff: cracked, reddened skin that itched and burned even before winter.

"I should probably pick up a few groceries this week to prepare for the storm. Are we all set with everything else? Let's see, there's a flashlight in the closet and that weather radio my parents gave us. What else?"

"It won't be that bad, sweets. I've seen worse." It's true; she had.

Max walked across the living room in two steps and sat before her laptop on their English Oak kitchen table. The table was a relic of the previous tenants who couldn't manage to angle the rectilinear monstrosity out the narrow doorframe and, thusly, left it behind with a note. They squeezed it in but couldn't reverse course. Exactly how this happened was a puzzle that often plagued Max when he sat there on sleepless nights. The piece was a blessing and a curse: It was simultaneously the most valuable accoutrement in their apartment (not to mention the only furniture that didn't require assembly) but was also the most ridiculous, stoutly looming dead center within the box layout of the apartment and occupying nearly the entire floor space of the kitchen. There was only a narrow mote of walking space on two sides of the table through which they could slip by, and there wasn't even enough room to fully extend the drawers. Opening two browsers, Max clacked away at the keyboard. Caroline poked at the remote until the TV flashed off and then rolled over on the couch, ceremonially ending her night. Max, by force of habit, opened his mouth and started to ask something that only escaped as "D'you wa?" before severing the thought and smacking his lips shut. Instead, he clicked on the second browser and snapped through a few menu options: balchao, barta, kofta, jhinga, saag—all these exotic names excited Max, and somehow his craving was inversely proportional to his understanding. The more cryptic descriptions like "pureed eggplant, light ghee" stoked his curiosity more so than the accessible "skewered chicken," which only cracked him up, as he imagined a Punjabi woman sneaking up on the poor caged bird and shanking it a dozen times before tossing it in a clay oven. Mulligatawny soup had always conjured for him an oddly specific image of a brunette porn star named Tawny Mulligan who had earned a reputation for flubbing sex scenes on the first take—to the wild amusement of the greasy crew.

Settling on a minced lamb kabob lathered in apricot chutney and rosemary naan bread for Caroline, Max returned to the first browser window. A trail of increasingly expensive flights from New York to New

Orleans burned before him on the screen. Still expensive—too expensive to broach the subject with Caroline, he mused, as if the cost had anything to do with it.

* * *

With the storm scheduled to strike the mid-Atlantic early in the week, Max had to move up his individual counseling session to Thursday in place of the usual Monday routine. The sky was still, betraying no knowledge of coming torrents except for the circling black-tipped gulls that swooned and choked out gasping cries. Much lower, and more aimless, the human beings patted over concrete, bobbing in and out of corner bodegas and espresso bars—greetings / goodbyes / grunted apologies all swirled into one hedonistic mass of palazzo trousers and rolled skinny jeans covering clammy legs that hopelessly swished up against one another. A white-haired Polish man sold hot dogs from a cart at the perimeter of McCarren Park adjacent to the train station. Max found it odd that he didn't sell kielbasa or at least bratwursts, but he bought two anyway. Not for hunger. Rather, he was feeling jittery and a shade nauseous from gulping three successive lattes during an afternoon meeting with Portia and wanted to blunt the feeling with fatty consumption. Her travel blog followers were up, way up, and her advertising income now afforded her more opportunities to offer her staff paid assignments—her staff consisting of Max and occasionally her boyfriend, Shlomo, a native New Yorker who could augment the experiences of the two southern transplants when the reviews involved neighborhoods outside of Brooklyn or Manhattan. It turns out that Portia Winchester, from old Raleigh Tobacco money, and Max Orbach, from the north Texas town of Martha and no particular status, were comically befuddled by the clannish enclaves of Queens that sprawled out past the end of the train line in Flushing: suburb-like yet somehow utterly alien to the brightly paved southern ones around which they had grown up.

The G train, characteristically shaky, was compounding Max's caffeine tremors and precluding any writing. Instead, he plotted out his session with Ramona at the United World Counseling Center. Could heart palpitations bomb a pee test? At his intake appointment weeks ago Yuri had asked about any physical symptoms of alcoholism.

"What do you mean? What could happen?"

"Like, do you get the shakes?" Yuri stretched out his hands like a sleepwalking mime.

"Oh. Then no." Max was relieved. He couldn't be that much of a train wreck if his body still held it together for the world to see.

Today his hands shook. But it was an occupational side-effect, born of the desire for energy, for tingly enthusiasm. Still, he wondered what Yuri would say about it if they crossed paths in the waiting room. Instead of Yuri, though, there were Angie and Marcus. The former sat upright on the emerald couch with her legs crossed and kind of squirmed, almost coyly, beneath her beige blouse. Marcus, who was ranting about something—names and places Max didn't recognize—acknowledged the smaller man warmly, the way a youth pastor beams dumbly at even the reluctant members of his flock. Always evasive toward men she couldn't read (those of a different social class) Angie was twirling her fried golden perm wave and feigning interest in the unattended social services window across the shared lobby.

"My man, what is up?" Marcus spoke as if they had a storied history, extending a meaty palm. His brassy alto timbre was somehow still distinctly masculine, just as his formless striped tee seemed noble even while sporting broad moons of moisture beneath his arm. Angie glanced up once then jerked her head downward toward her red clutch and fished for nothing in particular. Max noticed her clear cerulean eyes that clashed with the ashy streaks of mascara below. Her cheap, haughty glamour never failed to irk—and excite him. She looked, he had determined one day after protracted analysis, like Caroline would if she had continued drinking at the pace she did when they first met seven years ago.

"Just making a rare Thursday visit. My session with Ramona got moved up on account of the storm. How about you two?" Angie scooped up her phone and spasmodically swiped at the screen.

"Oh, Ramona! You lucky, she fine. That Sandy bitch on the other hand, that's gonna be nothin' to mess around with."

"Yeah, my wife and I should be alright, though. We live on the third floor and don't own any valuables. I just need to pick up some groceries for once in my life."

"Nah, I'm serious. The water from them storms is no joke. When I was a teenager—14, 15, something like that—the rain from Gloria flooded our family house.

Insurance wouldn't pay for shit. My parents fought like dogs after that. Always shouting. It was like they made such a habit of yelling at the insurance adjusters that they kept on going between the two of them. My daddy finally ended up heading down south, Carolina I think, for a month-long job. After about six months I came to my mama and said, 'he ain't coming back, is he?' She just turned around, dropped her laundry basket, and as she was walking away I heard, 'No, baby.' And that was that. Never saw him again and she never mentioned him again. Guess she decided she was better off murdering his memory than mourning a live ghost. All that started with a hurricane."

Angie, who had perked up at some point during Marcus's story, was applying coral lipstick with one hand and tracking her face on her phone screen with the other. Yuri had also peeked his round, unblinking face around the door to summon Max to Ramona's office. She didn't pop out herself. Must be preparing a piss cup, Max reasoned.

Before disappearing into the narrow wedge of light brought forth from the United World Counseling Center's inner office space, Max turned back to Marcus and said, "They do tend to set a lot of other events in motion. Hurricanes."

Ramona had straightened her hair today. For every other session it had been a dark luffa of curls radiating in every direction off her beaming face. This afternoon she looked sleek, more corporate than the "LCSW" that adorned her name. She glanced Max up and down, discreetly, the way a mother investigates a teenager in the wee hours of the morning. Her face was mostly shapeless but glossed by either some finishing spray or natural ardor into the sheen of chocolate mousse. She wore a purple chiffon dress that managed to draw out even more carats from the sparkling gold stack that weighed down her left hand. To Max she had previously been part of the machinery of the United World Counseling Center, an inquisitor to be placated with the correct answers. For their prior sessions she had worn loud wool sweaters that enveloped her body into a shapeless bubble, like a warbler. That her breasts competed valiantly beneath those squishy drapes did not go unnoticed by Max. Still, it was not until today that her face came into focus, her nose long and finely blunted into a round terminus, as one could imagine as a common Caribbean feature. Her office, purposefully sterile, sported a faux potted jade plant, folders, and white walls peppered with yellowish informational fliers. Thus, amid the desolation, Ramona looked silly, ornamental in her royal plumage.

"Max, sit down and tell me about your week. Or, well, just the last few days since our last date. Ha. Thanks for coming in ahead of schedule by the way— that storm." She flashed her teeth across the room. Younger counselors such as Ramona always had that polished habit of snuffing out exclamatory expressions before they ignited genuine excitement.

"Of course. My week's been fine." He honestly tried to survey the past few days but drew a blank. Caroline lying on the couch. Dinners—an endless sequentiality of meals that morphed together into starches and fatty carbohydrates. "I had group just last night, so I suppose that's fresh on my mind for once." She was dressed for someone, no doubt about it. But, for whom? The husband? No. She didn't seem like the date night on Thursday type.

"Well how was it—your group?" She crossed her legs and leaned back in her squeaky chair—simultaneously settling in for story-time and inviting Max into her space.

"Oh, it was a good time with donuts and coffee. No, I'm being serious. Some of those guys have the best stories, and I don't mean that in some sort of flippant way. Sadly, I have little to contribute that would be of any use to anyone in that room."

"That sounds all right." She stifled a giggle. Was it a giggle? "What I was asking, though, was about the topic. What did Yuri ask you to share?" Must have been a rogue giggle, for now she was overcorrecting. Everything about her was tidy today, including the desk's simpering stacks of neatly aligned paper edges. In the corner of the jamocha-wood-finish desk were a pair of comically conspicuous white latex gloves. It was a mocking reminder of what's to come, a rubbery protection against the dissolution of roles.

"Right, right. He asked us to reflect upon our support systems and discuss how our transgressions (not his word) have impacted said individuals."

"Ok, wonderful. And, what did you have to say? Who constitutes your support system?

"I didn't really get to talk much. Brought up Caroline, but we ran out of time and kind of adopted a rapid-fire sort of thing with those of us who were slow on the draw."

"Well, sure, but I'm asking you now to share with me. Caroline's your wife, right? Is she your basis of support?"

"Yes," he began—the word gingerly patting the room as a cat's paw tests for safety. "She would love for me to continue not drinking." Tearful shouts, scattershot accusations, his reddened face stinging from a slap, brown liquor poured into the sink.

"That's great to hear." Ramona beamed, likely not in appreciation of his words but more as an encouragement to keep fleshing out the subject. "But, do you feel that she gives you the strength to continue with your recovery?"

"She—" Max straightened up in his chair, finding his voice. "She does, yes. Absolutely."

Caroline's childish palm struck him with only a glancing blow, but the cold shame of the Atlantic wind burned on his cheek. Lights flicked on within a rectilinear apartment building just steps away.

"I'm out. Good luck with life." Max pivoted and began to walk toward the corner subway station, knowing full well that her steps would soon overtake him. Her outstretched hand clawed at him, trying to hook him by the shoulder and reel him back to her amid shrieking sobs. But Max, fearing that the scene would be misinterpreted by the inevitable arbitrators (neighbors, maybe cops), began a sprint with the correct assumption that he could outduel her bony legs, even drunk. He pattered against the pavement in loafers that felt paper thin against the icy pavement, running wildly past the L station until finding himself at the Greenpoint G. Jumped off at the first stop in Queens— funny how crossing the rivers and creeks that divvy up New York City always seems to carry a psychic weight. Spotted a swanky neighborhood bar glowing neon red across a black street, smoothed his overgrown sprouts

of wavy hair, wiped a few stagnant puddles of sweat on his brow (minimal thanks to the chilled air), and crossed over.

"Max, we haven't yet been able to talk about Caroline, I mean *really* talk about her. Tell me what you love about your wife?" Ramona shifted a little in her seat and rubbed her hands together. Somehow, with that sly, barely perceptible way that beautiful women often carry as a sort of birthright, she shifted her head so that her gold-plated earrings jangled together and shimmered with spectral bursts of afternoon light.

"This may sound strange, but well, I'm going to just say it anyway. Women—and by the way please don't interpret this as some chauvinistic confirmation of gender roles—a woman loves the man. Like, she really loves the man for what role, what existential place he holds in her day to day life."

"Max, you're veering off course. Let's focus on your personal situation and not society at large."

"No, I'm acquitting myself poorly at the moment, but I do assure you that this applies to Caroline and me. Let me try again: You see, a woman loves her man, but a man loves the conception of himself that he sees through the eyes of his woman. Thus, women are lovers, givers. Men are narcissists."

"But now you're speaking in generalities; that's always dangerous ground to be treading on, Max. Besides, to be a lover one has to find a willing and equal partner in the form of another lover, so don't women and their men both have to be lovers—'givers' as you say?"

Max, though he didn't dare break character, smiled within himself, pleased that he had plied Ramona from her course.

The steady red blaze of the sign betrayed an agitated flickering up close. Flanked on either side by bronze Marseille faux lanterns that burned a sallow orange, the sizzling script spelled out a family name— perhaps Italian, but it didn't really matter, being the type of spruced up plucky little joint that would reincarnate every other year under a different theme, a different brand. Spying an opening at the polished cherry wood bar, Max snaked his way through the crowd and sidled up next to a red-haired woman who was shouting something vulgar at the younger bartender. She was a few years older than Max, maybe mid to late thirties, and wore a black cape dress and Burberry suede boots. Her crimped hair bounced carelessly as she theatrically gulped a shot, abruptly clanking the glass back down on the bar. At first she seemed unaffected by this new male presence beside her, holding court from her corner post among the regulars. The clean cut 20-something bartender, sharply handsome beneath his bleached white bistro shirt, regarded her cautiously but with amusement—the way one greets a Rottweiler at a dog park.

"Who the hell are you?" She flipped first only her head toward Max, then slid the rest of her body around to squarely face him.

"Tabitha, seriously? Not cool to scare off my customers." The bartender temporarily abandoned a group at the other end of the bar. He was thin, slightly short of stature with compactly taut muscles that he highlighted with his fitted shirt being a size too small. His naturally curly black hair crowned his head with an unctuous rigidity while his olive face gave way to dark

*protuberances beneath his eyes. Face to face he seemed
closer to Max's age.* "Hey, man. Don't listen to this
one." *He gestured his head toward the woman.* "What
can I get for you?"

"Fuck you, Blake. He knows I'm messing with
him." *To Max:* "You know I'm messing with you, guy.
You fuckin know that, don't look so sheepish, you're
among friends here. Take a shot with me?"

"Sure, a shot sounds right. I'm Max—" *And then,*
"That's who the hell I am."

Whooping laughter. "Ha, Blake I like this guy. Get
us a round of whiskey, doubles, with chasers. Max here
needs to catch up if he wants to be of any use." *She
extended a pale arm from beneath her folds of flowy
fabric.* "I'm Tabitha. Blake's the best bartender in
Queens. I love that guy, seriously he's the best! What
brings you here? Live in the neighborhood?"

"Pleasure to meet you, and no just wandered in.
Shitty day."

"Aww, I'm sorry, babe." *She cooed
absentmindedly.* "My day sucked too. Do you know I
was stood up? Supposed to meet some dude from
OKCupid, arrived early to catch up with Blake and the
guys and have a couple drinks while waiting, but two
hours later and the guy's a no-show so I just hung out
here anyway. It's usually all regulars during the week,
so I pretty much know everyone."

"I'm impressed."

"Yeah you are." *Her eyes flared like stoked coals.*

*They finished their drinks and ordered another
round. Tabitha, whose curiosity had thus far been
occupational—like bus drivers who wave at each other
in passing—now combed over his whole form with her*

eyes.

*"I see you have a ring, married or something?"
She asked it in a bouncy way that offered immunity to
any malleable response the question could evoke.*

*"Yeah, I suppose I am. Wanna hear some shit? My
wife's sleeping with her boss."*

*"Sucks, poor baby." She squeezed his thigh and
blinked her eyes.*

*"I mean, I don't have a smoking gun or anything,
but I'm pretty sure. Something's going on at least."*

*"You have to trust your instincts with these things.
Gotta rely on yourself--hone in on you and shut every
dissenting opinion out—only way to live." She thumped
a hand against her chest, jangling a whole system of
costume necklaces. "That's always been my personal
rule for living. It applies to sex too." She had been
examining Max's lips as if trying to divine some greater
truth through their stillness. "Blake, we need more
whiskey!"*

"Sex? I'm afraid I don't follow."

*"If you don't shut out everything else and
concentrate on your own pleasure, then you aren't
really going to enjoy it. Then you're just acting for the
other person, which is a pretty shitty thing to do. It
seems nice and considerate and all—you know, to fake
it for the sake of some poor sap's ego—but that's just
cheapening the whole experience. Get it?"*

*They each drank another shot of whiskey and then
two more rounds of beer. Max felt evacuated from his
life and placed outside of time into this sanctuary. It
didn't feel cruel at all to ignore the buzzing in his front
pocket. Tabitha had scooted her chair up against his
and draped her arm across the back of his studded*

seatback. Her arm looked muscular, but its bigness was exacerbated by the sallow glow of weak pigmentation amid the dim lighting.

The restrooms were tucked away beside a berth at the base of the stairs that descended downward into some sort of basement. Tabitha shoved him into a tiny stall in the women's room that could barely accommodate the two of them, even standing pressed together. She kissed him without hesitation, as if they were old lovers kept away from each other's affections for some duration. Max noticed for the first time that she was tall, nearly his height, which physically diminished the distance between their mouths. Somehow Max interpreted the effortlessness of the action as cosmic approval, and he forcibly darkened the pathways of his mind that burned, even after being doused in liquor, with nagging examination.

The intermittent buzzing evolved into a constant hum against his thigh, abated only when he dropped his pants to the floor to allow Tabitha's hand easier access. It wouldn't be until later that he would read, amid countless frantic messages, one saying, "I swear to you nothing at all happened!! I don't know why you had to say such an awful thing to me." Having freed him from his boxers, Tabitha's hand began a greedy motion. It was coarse and sloppy and all they could muster within the confinement. Suddenly Max became acutely aware of the awful fluorescent pallor and could smell the sterile sweetness of urinal cakes. He brushed her aside, dressed, and ascended the stairs to drink another beer and then close his tab.

Turning his phone off, he wandered out into the numb chill of winter night, wind simultaneously cooling *his flesh and warming his capillaries.*

Outside of the United World Counseling Center the wind whistled past Max, smelling faintly of verbena. The slap of the cool breeze blended oddly with the wet heat of the sun staring down at him through only a gossamer cloud cover. Before climbing the steps to the elevated train platform, he stepped into the Starbuck's below and ordered coffee and mineral water. The coffee, which seemed to bake within the cardboard and induce an aroma of pizza crust, steamed out of the plastic lid opening and nearly seared his lip upon first inspection. Instead, he began with the beaded green glass bottle that was slippery to the touch. He imagined he was drinking pale beer from a sweaty balcony overlooking Bourbon Street—carelessly diving into a New Orleans night. If he were standing on such a balcony, Max reasoned, he wouldn't actually be holding a glass bottle. They would have 32 ounce plastic cups stacked by the exit to pour bottles into. At their favorite joint, Bourbon Street Blues Company, Max and his old buddy from high school, Sam Eaglin, would snatch up bottles of cheap light beer that were offered at three for the price of one upstairs. Then, since simple mathematics didn't allow for three 12 ounce bottles to fit within one 32 ounce cup, they would chug one beer and only pour the remaining two. It had taken a few trips to the city, but eventually they had the French Quarter figured out, everything had a science to it. They knew which hotel in the Garden District served a free breakfast buffet in the morning and just how to sneak past the front desk that conveniently faced the composed flow of name badges from the Convention Center and only could peripherally spy the dining room.

They knew what side street taverns served legitimate bowls of crawfish étoufée unassumingly bathing in brown roux and priced for locals. They knew, too, what bars girls favored past 2 AM.

He thought back to his conversation with Ramona and what he had said, or rather not said, about Caroline. Always, it seemed, that he was toting around a bag of unused phrases after counseling sessions. A list of thoughts, like souls in the ephemera waiting to be born, lingered around him, and somehow there was never time for more than one or two to emerge. What he had wanted to say about Caroline this time, a thought that had been marinating in his head for years, was this: how men use words literally and women use them not so much for their actual meaning but to prod—to produce an effect in the listener like a fireplace poker stoking barely glowing coals into wild flames. He couldn't say it, though. Not just because Ramona had bitten off their session early in order to send him crawling into the bathroom with a plastic cup. He couldn't pair this statement about the men/women binary with his other generality. One such comment spiked the conversation, but two would have appeared loaded—as if he had been carrying around a full belly of misogynistic conclusions that he spewed all over her desk. The truth is that he had been thinking a great deal about the machinery of communication between men and women, but his interest had been professional rather than emotional. He wanted to understand from a distance—to continue conversations that he had had with male friends (mainly Sam) for years. None of this was really about Caroline in particular, he lied, while testing again the coffee.

He would go to New Orleans in December. He would go with Sam and he would drink. By then his piss-cup probation will have ended, and if Caroline wanted to declare war, so be it. Her decision. Did he still reside in the margins of her grace, or had that finally dried up with his arrest? He would go and discover.

* * *

The weather radio buzzed with continual computerized loops that warned of risks to the various flood zones, the indifference of the alien voice serving only to further confirm their human fears. Caroline and Max were still seated on the couch, alternatively looking at each other and the vast blackness of the square window. Normally the Citi building in Queens was visible from their vantage point, but its radiance had either been blotched out by the storm or power across the Newtown Creek had been lost. It amazed Max to consider that any such structure, massive, global, could be knocked unconscious by a storm. Caroline laughed out loud when Max told her of his surprise. Growing up in north Texas, storms to him meant tornadoes, and these only seemed to truly punish the rural areas: isolated farmhouses, mobile homes, RVs, etc. God's judgment was decisive across the lonely plains, while city-dwellers faced only the scrutiny of man's law. That was the covenant. Of course, as he well knew, hurricanes were a different matter—the most egalitarian of the storms, and he looked back from the nothingness in the window to the tired lines under Caroline's active eyes. The cable had already gone out (the last blurb they saw on NY1 begging viewers not to call 911) and the lights were now flickering. Rain crashed in sheets across the thin double pane of the window, which rattled and hissed.

"We better move to the kitchen and shut all the doors in case the glass breaks," said Caroline.

At the roughened oak table within their windowless room, and at the center of the box apartment amid closed doors to all other rooms, they sat opposite one another like rival generals in the war room. A low hum, not of compressors shifting on but something more ghostly, penetrated the walls and engulfed them. The window screamed at the rain like a scorned harpy.

"Caroline, look, I'm going to just be honest with you. Sam really needs someone to go back to New Orleans with him, so I think I'm going to go only for a few days in December."

"Don't you dare," began Caroline, eyes burning black, "don't you dare bring up that city now of all times."

"I'm sorry, I wasn't really thinking about that. I—" He groped for the right word before she could continue her devastation. "I just wanted to put it out there before it grows into this whole problem—again."

"That means you're going to be drinking again. Fucking great!" She slapped the table. "And he doesn't need you to go. You go because you want to go. Admit it! You're not taking care of anyone but yourself, and you tend to do a pretty shitty job of that."

"I'll be done with treatment by then, and I don't plan to really drink—not much anyway. Listen, I don't expect you to understand, but there's simply unfinished business in that city." Again, he had been careless with his words. Her smallness was punctuated by dilated eyes, and though he was only of average size, he felt swollen, oafish, ridiculous. He thought about everything she had been through—only seven years since her family had been scattered, her house destroyed, graduate school plans abandoned. And what was the payoff? Being with him? He had treated her badly. Her eyes still smoldered across from him, but in that moment he felt only a surge of compassion toward her. Then with a holy shake, the power zapped off.

* * *

Max had always imagined that experiencing a hurricane would be for everyone the way it was for weather reporters and storm chasers: rain coats, hats flying off, clinging desperately to a stop sign. In reality it had been wrought with the passive sense of waiting, dry and lost within inert walls—more like being stuck in an elevator. The wreckage was evident throughout Brooklyn, as the couple surveyed their neighborhood the next morning. They didn't speak much to each other except to note fallen overhead signs from businesses, glass blown inward, collapsed streetlights. They were lucky. The neighborhoods of north Brooklyn— Williamsburg, Greenpoint, and Bushwick—were largely spared. Meanwhile, the coastlines of Staten Island and the Rockaways were wiped clean. Even their fragile little window somehow held its form. By contrast, industrial floor-to-ceiling high-rise windows in lower Manhattan had shattered mercilessly and sent jagged pieces like shrapnel at the few workers unlucky enough to have remained.

Caroline spoke first: "Well, by the sound of things last night, I thought we'd be washed away. But this isn't so bad, just some garbage blown about and a few fallen signs—they won't be missed. I've certainly seen worse." It was true, she had. She gestured toward the broken arm of a London planetree beside the sidewalk, but Max couldn't see the deep cracks that detached it from the trunk. It was temporarily buoyed by a bed of leaves below, awaiting now just a gentle breeze to finally liberate it.

They fell silent for a while, walking slowly to nowhere with heads low and close together. At one point Max reached for her hand, but Caroline tenderly brushed him off. "Don't," she said.

"We're going to be OK. We *are*." He elongated "are" into two syllables—the latter dropping off a bit. "I'm sorry that I upset you before, Caroline. You have to understand that it's not about you, not a big deal at all, it's just a little excursion with a buddy and then we'll be back to normal, you and I, I mean."

"Wow, you've got it all figured out, don't you? Nothing's ever 'a big deal' to you, is it?"

"I never *said* that I had it—"

"Stop." She raised her hand like a traffic control cop. "You've said plenty. You know what's funny? Now that I think about it, I've never before been left for a city—my own hometown no less."

"Jesus, Caroline, you act like I'll never be back. It's just a goddamn weekend trip."

"Don't say anything." Then after some time, Answer one question for me: Why am I not enough?"

27

2002

The fluorescent wash of the overhead casing shone eerily on the newly scrubbed glass countertop that held within it a folksy exhibit of pipes—everything from corncobs to hand-carved Corsican briar Rinaldis. Thursdays were when the regulars would pick up their pouches of cut tobacco, and the cigar consiglieres would strut about the walk-in humidor on Saturday afternoons. Today was a Tuesday, and not a soul had deigned to enter the store in nearly two hours—not counting fellow mall employees who popped in for a pack of Marlboros or the squat carnival barker from the T-Mobile kiosk who waddled in periodically to stretch his legs and evade bed sores on his ass from the flat steel stool. Walter, having just stamped out a cigarette before it even burned down to the butt, his third of the afternoon, meandered out of the humidor and back into the storefront. He was tall and thin, bald except for a tuft of white that formed a perfect semi-circle around his liver-spotted dome, and he wore button-down flannel that his physique could have perhaps filled a couple decades ago.

"Well, Max, we've got to get you a little closer to the schedule." He regarded the much younger man with a cautious sideways glance, being uncomfortable around the newer generation, especially the college-educated stock that to him seemed to be cropping up everywhere and snatching silly degrees on their parents' dime. In Walter's youth the legacy families sent their sons to places like Austin or private colleges in the Northeast. The really smart kids, Walter reasoned, apprenticed to become plumbers or electricians. It irked him to see the enrollment at regional state universities, the type chartered first as quaint normal colleges, bloated by middle-class matriculants into provincial research centers.

"You were 30 minutes late today," added Walter, turning away from his employee and toward the unencumbered entrance out to the mall's main drag.

"Yeah, I'm sorry, Walt." Max stifled a yawn. "My roommate blocked me in the driveway and I couldn't back out. I hope you didn't get too busy without me."

"Shit, no. This place has been quieter than a whorehouse on Sunday." They each pushed out a chuckle. Walter was often salty until an unfamiliar face appeared in the store or a regular's wife came to chaperone. To those who didn't know him, he was ex-Navy, which was true only to the extent that he frequented the VFW where he enjoyed flirting with the widows.

Walter sighed audibly and shifted his weight from

leg to leg before wincing and leaning backward against the high cherry wood shelf that housed pre-bagged tobacco with customer names scribbled by a Sharpie. Hemorrhoids, Max assumed, wondering whether they were supposed to throb or itch—or just kind of sizzle. No, it was definitely some form of pain, he thought, remembering a Preparation H commercial that had come on the other night during a *Seinfeld* rerun. Old farts like Walt were always getting these aches and pains, but how bad could they really be if an over-the-counter cream could just disappear into the skin and win a microscopic battle with inflammation? Max caught himself tracing imaginary rectilinear shapes across the glass case, leaving an unctuous trail of fingerprints behind. After two squirts of Windex he circled the rag methodically, obscuring the evidence. Finding an odd serenity in the organic motion—akin to sweeping one's palms down the supple midsection of a girl—he began to scrutinize the other parts of the long counter for imperfections, squeezing out liquid here and there and eagerly buffing until the refulgent overhead panels winked back at him via the glass.

"Had your first shift cigarette?" asked Walter, noticing the shorter man's compulsivity.

"No, Walt, I'm fresh out. I was going to buy a pack of Camels when I got in today, but I'm a little short on cash."

"Here," said Walter, handing him a crisp box of Camel Lights. "Payday's Friday."

"Thanks."

The humidor cycled in moisture to augment the stale mall atmosphere and the dry cinders of a Texas summer under dying August light. Max breathed in the woodlands amalgam of earthy musk—cigars wafting off leather oak and blending richly with the bright scents of cedar strips. All of this seemed to him so much cleaner than the gray plume straying from between his fingers. It took him seven minutes to finish a cigarette, so he reasoned that by elongating the gap between drags he could stretch his break out to eight—nine minutes with some discipline. Of course, this method lent itself to daydreaming, and soon Max's mind wandered off to a phone call earlier in the afternoon.

"Walt, do you know who's working this weekend?" he asked before clocking out and after dumping the ash trays and vacuuming the cosmetic strip of carpet that lay, coarse and flint-colored, between the entrance and the glass counter—the remainder of the carpet being sufficiently unemployed as to discreetly host errant soot or flecks of mud.

"Oh, let's see what we got here." He squinted at the *Romeo Y Julieta* calendar on the wall. "Looks like we got you—and—the Andys." Actually, only one of the pair went by "Andy." The other was Andrew, but as Walter's least favorite employee, his identity was purely a matter of managerial whims. Andy, on the other hand, was Walter's paragon of manhood—the son he imagined he would have had if his own hadn't been brainwashed by his bitch mom. After turning down an offer to play Single A ball for the Padres and then similarly spurning a scholarship to stay in town and play for Atena State, he began a career as an Assistant Manager for Wal-Mart, working evenings and weekends at Tobacco Bazaar. Tall and blond, he was the type of man who grew up propelled by slaps on the

back and "attaboys" from the previous generation's
elder statesmen—the kind of guy who wears shorts on
every single off day and despises collared or fitted
shirts. His wife was plump and short, but her meaty
frame, softened by good old-fashioned southern fare
like Frito pies and ambrosia, was balanced by her
penchant for flashy orange lipstick and youthful eyes
that danced from side to side when she worked a room.
The two of them spoke with a disarming country twang
that bent words upward at their corners, and they
sprinkled in just enough grammatical irregularities to
let you know they weren't trying to pull anything over
on anybody ("we was fixin' to load the truck").

Andrew was a corpulent nullity who had failed out
of Atena State a decade earlier but remained in town
ever since, paralyzed by his own promises to one day
"finish up and move away from all these fucktards." He
claimed to coach his eight-year-old daughter's soccer
team, but no one could really imagine that hulking mass
flopping up and down the pitch.

"So, I hate to ask this, but do you think there's any
way we could manage as a skeleton crew—just the
Andys?" asked Max, knowing full well the answer.

It was past ten when Max left the mall parking lot,
but the temperature still hadn't dropped below the 90s,
meaning he had to drive with the windows down. The
compressor had first flagged, then later died utterly, a
summer before, and he hadn't seen any sense in using a
month's worth of wages to invest in a 13-year-old
Camry. The rush of wind obscured some bouncy pop
alto on the radio. Christina Aguilera, Max thought to
himself, before recognizing that he hadn't really kept
track of the superstar sexpots the way he had his first

couple years of college. The CD player was jammed, having recently swallowed a Blink-182 album and not yet regurgitated it. He drove past the loop that circles Atena like a concrete halo, penetrating the innards of the town along Letheland Boulevard toward the town square. The downtown passage was an indulgence rather than a direct path to their rented house across Pegasus Drive from the college. But, on select summer nights, under the still glowing embers of fading August sky, Max liked to drive atop the scorched pavement—heat lingering from a violent Texas sun—and pass by the strings of yellow lights that draped the courthouse, illuminating the southward-facing Confederate soldier. There were two dive bars on the square, one poolhall, and a slightly less dive-y lounge that served as a happy hour haven for the neighboring law offices. All the bars were dead. It was a bland Tuesday night for the professionals in town, and the Atena State students were mostly gone until the fall semester began, which was still weeks away. The summer students were also largely missing, the last session having concluded the Thursday before with late term graduation the subsequent Saturday and all the usual fanfare of drab robes, rectilinear hats, and faux degrees that were actually letters announcing the timetable for legitimate diplomas to arrive in the mail. Max was among those who marched to much applause across that stage, though his cheering section of three (his parents and a nervous girlfriend) could hardly compete with the foghorn instrumental accompaniment of "Ashley"—something who came before.

Turning off Pecan, one of the two main drags that ran parallel to each other through the square, he passed the sole all-night coffee shop in town, Pluto's. Street lamps glowed a spectral pallor like swamp gas, which cast penumbras speckled by June bugs. Within the limbo between academic terms there were only a couple puffy-eyed graduate students smoking at the cast-iron sidewalk tables.

The house was a low-roofed ranch home built in the Fifties and periodically updated by the owners, whomever they were, into a mishmashed mausoleum of architectural zeitgeist across the decades. Short, stubby faux Doric columns had been implanted across the narrow band of cement serving as a porch, sneeringly protruding like buck teeth. Wan vinyl siding clung around three of the four exterior walls—the posterior remaining naked. Benson's bedroom, the only true living quarters, sported thick shag carpeting that was nearly impossible to vacuum. Max's bedroom, meant originally as the servant's pantry, had only cement for a floor.

"Hey-O, Max. You've got some messages. Also, Sam called like three more times, so I guess we should probably give him an answer, huh?"

"I'll call him tonight. Looks like I'm covered for this weekend. Are we taking the truck, or what's the plan?"

"Aww shit—let's make Sam drive."

Max shook his head. "He's being a dick about it. Said he just made a road trip in the Accord and doesn't want to pile on the miles."

"Fuck, I'm not driving again. We took the truck to Padre Island and it sucked. You two idiots are terrible navigators, and you caked sand all over the floorboards. What about your piece of shit?"

"Really?"

"Oh, right. Air conditioner. You need to fix that shit, son!"

"Get real." Max wandered passed Benson, who returned to his PlayStation, into the kitchen and the blinking green light of the answering machine. An 800 number had called twice—spaced exactly an hour apart.

"Hello, this is a very important message for Max Orbach. Please call us back at—" Delete. The sweet feminine voice almost lulled him to hear it through. Almost. There are limits.

There were, just as Benson had said, precisely three incoming calls from Sam Eaglin. Their intervals, Max noted with some amusement, were nearly as even as the debt collector's. The light continued to blink, as there remained one last message.

"Max, hey it's me—um, it's Jessica. Call me when you get home from work. I was hoping maybe I could come over or whatever. So—call me when you get this. Bye. Oh, love you. Bye."

Snatching one of Benson's beers from the fridge, he found first his bedroom and then the crumpled soft pack of Camels in his pocket. Max hated soft packs but couldn't exactly whine about it, given the circumstances. He stripped down to boxers and a pit-stained white undershirt, then lay supine on the bed with the lit cigarette dangling out the side of his lips— channeling James Dean or some such 50s stud. They always seemed to battle cigarettes with such ease, as if they've been thrust into their gaping mouths and now must be dominated before moving on with their cursed, pretty lives.

Finally snuffing out the tan butt into a stolen glass

ashtray atop the nightstand—an artifact of sorts to commemorate a booze-fueled morning at Denny's when he'd finally won the waitress's phone number—he sat up and chugged the rest of the beer.

First he called Sam. No answer. So, he slipped back into the kitchen where he could spy Benson in the living room cursing at NFL Blitz and nodding his head along to a live version of Ice Cube's "Fuck tha Police" on the stereo. Reassured, Max grabbed two more bottles, and then two more.

Jessica answered on the first ring. "Max, did you get off work late? We're still going to hangout, right?"

"Yeah, I just got home. I'm kind of tired, Jess. Wanna come over and have a beer?"

When her little hand was heard pattering on the door and reaching Max's ears as the hollow crack of a mini conga, he scurried to the living room, hoping to usher her to the back of the house before locking into a three-way conversation with Benson. Max seated her next to him on the edge of the bed and clicked up the volume on the TV a few notches.

"Beer?"

She accepted one, twisted off the top and gulped for several seconds.

"Sorry, I didn't mean to chug it, but it's so hot out—still—makes me thirsty."

"It's fine," Max chuckled. I have another one for you when you're ready."

Max examined her for a moment, the bare dangling legs, the dark hair yanked back into a ponytail by a simple black band, the narrow face flushed by the heat, the half-starved torso that somehow failed to fill out an extra small "System of a Down" t-shirt. Her features, smeared shadowy beneath her eyes to match clumps of eyeliner, were pretty enough, Max considered, despite a weak jaw line. He remembered the upcoming weekend and was for a moment filled with love—her recessed chin becoming an exotic adaptation rather than a flaw.

"I missed you today, baby!" Jess began. She twisted open a fresh beer and contorted herself on the bed into an Indian-style posture, facing Max directly. "Did you miss me? You never called me last night before bed like you said you would."

"Oh, Jess I'm sorry about that, fell asleep. I love you, babe." He leaned in and kissed her, lingering there until she pulled back.

"Wait a second," she smiled, the darkness of her pupils swollen into something like black poker chips. "Is it OK if I finish my beer?" She had over half of the bottle left, but she dispensed of it with ease, beaming as does a gymnast who has just stuck a dismount. He resumed his probing of her mouth and had just begun pawing at her breasts over the t-shirt when they were startled by a knock at the door.

"All righty, we can take the truck to Austin, Max. But, we're making Sam drive his God damn car from there." Benson stood there dumbly in the doorway for a minute staring at Max, before comprehending his misstep. "Oh, sorry, hey Jessica. OK, OK, I'll leave y'all alone—about to head off to bed anyway." Benson stomped away, stopping apparently at the refrigerator before cursing and slamming his bedroom door.

"What's going on?" Jessica asked, standing. "Are you really going to Austin?"

"Um, yeah, but just to meet up with Sam." He faltered, searching her black eyes for a moment. "Then we're driving to New Orleans from there."

"What the fuck, why didn't you mention this earlier? And Sam? What would he even have to talk about for a whole road trip?"

"I just found out that I'm covered for work this weekend. I didn't think I'd be able to go, so I didn't want to worry you for nothing."

"Oh, so you guys have been planning this for a while?"

"Nah, a few days. Look, what's the big fucking deal? It's a road trip—guys do it all the time. Sam went out to New Orleans with some UT buddies a week ago."

"It's fine." She lowered her eyes and her shoulders went limp within her t-shirt. "I'm going to miss you, that's all. We never take vacations together, and I've been telling you for a year that I want to visit my sister in San Antonio."

"We'll go, babe. I promise. After my next paycheck." He closed in around her torso and kissed her forehead. Their lips met tentatively before she pulled back.

"So. Why *is* Sam going back to New Orleans, if he *was* just there a week ago?" There was something about the cadence of her voice that was off. He knew just enough to recognize that but not enough to know what to do with the information. It was like certain critical neuropathways in his brain hadn't yet been properly soldered together.

"Don't know—that's Sam for you. Ben and I never really know what's up with him. Knowing him, it'll be pretty tame, nothing for you to worry about."

She took a step back and regarded him from a

distance. "I never said I was worried about anything, but now I feel like I should be. That guy's just weird, that's all. I'm disappointed, OK? Did you remember about my cousin's wedding on Saturday? I guess you're not going anymore."

"Oh, Jess, I'm sorry. I'm going to have to miss that."

"You never spend time with my family. You're always—I feel—you know what? It's fine. Go and have fun. Please, though, please spend some time with me when you get back and maybe take me to San Antonio, OK?" Regardless of the sister, she always seemed fixated on the Alamo. Perhaps she's just drawn to lost causes, he thought.

"Of course, babe. I swear to you I will," he said, wondering how long he could go on like this.

Back at Martha High School Sam had been an oddity to outsiders, which was nearly everyone, and a frustration to his closest friends. The Eaglins were fixtures at the nondenominational megachurch out by the old state highway that led toward Atena. The two north Texas towns were only separated by about 25 miles of roadway that was flanked by scraggily stretches of plains hosting only occasional bur oaks and one Diamond Shamrock gas station. A few construction cones stood insistently on the horizon with paved residential partitions that served, then, as merely paper streets for a generation not yet come of age. Owing to his family's asceticism Sam didn't drink or smoke, a nuisance to the other members of their little clique. He rarely cussed and generally avoided even the mild scandal of sneaking into an R-rated movie. Mild-tempered to a fault, back then, he seemed totally unaffected when, in the last six weeks grading period of their senior year, he was overtaken by Elva Cisneros and graduated salutatorian. Whether it was some firmly planted Puritan DNA or an acquired performance of stoicism, his true nature was obscured behind squinty eyes that were blown up to cartoonish proportions by huge slabs of prescription glass within a rectilinear tortoise shell frame. In the ways of women he seemed to both Max and Benson—and the fourth member of their group, Travis Kim—to be asexual at best. Of course, none of them pressed this point too strongly, considering that of the four only Travis had so much as touched female genitalia by graduation, and even his conquest hardly registered with the others and their bizarre expectations of women, being Lucia Negrescu, a Romanian exchange student who gained nearly 50 pounds on an American diet and never really adapted to the post-grunge styles of the late 90s. So, it surprised Max when one Saturday, after a movie (rated R but Benson had lied to lure Sam to the theater where he was captive without a car and felt no moral compunction to leave, having come not of his own volition), the two of them stood outside Max's house under the only street lamp for half a mile and discussed Sam's "courtship" of a sophomore flautist.

"Andrea? Nah, never heard of her," admitted Max. "Wait, unless you mean Andi—Andi Springer. Christ, no one calls her 'Andrea'—if that's who you mean."

"Um, yeah, Andi. Yes, her name is Andi," declared Sam as if he were showing off a newly adopted pet.

"OK, well sure, she's cute and all—long dark hair—wears it in a ponytail with a scrunchy thing, I think. Wait, isn't she going out with Colt Carter?"

"Technically, yeah. But she doesn't know him really. If she did there's just no way she would—what I mean is she's seeing him for the wrong reasons, which I'm sure on some level she knows, and besides—well, look, it's a complicated problem; I know that. You see, though, I—I have a history with her."

"*You* have a history?" Max said it rudely with inordinate emphasis on the *you*. Recognizing this, he softened his tone. "OK, cool, well what exactly does this history entail?"

"Two years ago. On the bus, when our church youth group was riding to Mexico, she laid her head on my lap. Think about it, she willingly put her head that near to my—you know."

"Oh. Well shit, sounds like an open and shut case to me. Obviously she wanted to blow you right in front of God and everyone. What a skanky little lassie she is."

"Screw. You. Clearly you've never been with a woman because you don't understand even the finest minutia of how they—"

"Whoa, whoa, whoa, what exactly do you mean by 'been with a woman' because you sure as hell haven't either?"

"I mean 'been near' as in proximity—a more literal sense than your cretinous euphemisms would allow."

"OK, whatever, doesn't matter. Don't go all *Dawson's Creek* on me."

"I only watch it for Katie Holmes and you know that."

"Anyway—so what's happened lately with Andi? What are the recent developments?"

Sam blinked a few times and creased his eyebrows

as if he didn't understand the question. "I mean, we sit at the same table during B-lunch—some days they sit with us anyway, so we talk. It's a slow play kind of thing."

"By 'they' you mean she and Colt, right?"

"Damn it!" Sam spun around and threw his arms up theatrically and swayed to his car door. He nearly punctuated his rant by pounding a balled-up fist on the roof but paused midair, remembering the merchandise below. A few weeks earlier, Sam had been daydreaming his way to a red light and plowed into the curved ranch hand steel bumper of a Silverado. The aluminum fender of his own '88 Berretta was badly crumpled, while the truck barely knew it'd been struck. Ultimately the damage to Sam's car was superficial, but his parents still felt that they had endangered their only son with a feeble old junker and deigned that God had worked his will for a shiny new car via the accident. Thus, Sam now drove a glossy '98 Accord.

He pivoted slowly, as if hobbled, the way an old World War II veteran would have turned toward a pimply kid who'd asked him about liberating Auschwitz. Washed by the pale flickering green of the mercury vapor above, Sam visibly squashed patches of soft buffalo grass underfoot while ambling back to Max. The eerie syncopation of the flickering was made more unsettling by the bloodless pallor of the green light. Years earlier the city of Martha had resolved to replace all the mid-century streetlights with more efficient high-pressure sodium bulbs but had not yet bothered a few forgotten corners of the old neighborhood near the center of town—focusing instead on the subdivisions of red brick houses near the beige, newly minted shopping centers or the older (but still chic) mall, which even Dallasites from an hour south enjoyed.

"Well," began Sam. "What about you and Kristin? What's the plan there? I guess what I mean is—how does one take the next step?"

"You mean sex?"

"No! That's not—no, I'm just wondering what the strategy is to make things official, to make a particular lady into a girlfriend."

"I wish I knew, Sam. I—" Max sighed, feeling only slightly sorry for himself but mostly like a brother who has to deflate a sibling's belief in Santa Claus or the Tooth Fairy. "There's nothing between Kristin and me anymore, I don't think. I've been hopeful, believe me, but we've never really gotten off the ground."

"But, you went to Homecoming with her! And we all heard her making fun of what's her name, the chubby girl, who wrote you the letter. She likes you, right? There's no way—just no—she must have feelings for you. We all heard her—the letter—she was doing that nasally voice and reading it in front of everyone before first period. We heard it," he repeated triumphantly like a carpenter giving one final whack to the head of a nail.

"Dude, *did*. She *did* like me, but I'm pretty sure I blew it months ago. I didn't even kiss her the night of Homecoming. You see, girls give you a moment when they like you. A pitch down the middle. But, your timing has to be just right to connect with the sweet spot and knock it out of the park. You flinch at all and then you're late with the swing. Strike three. Now, as much as it pains me to think about it, I'm pretty sure she's screwing that James guy. Probably inflicting her cruel mockery on other girls for *his* benefit now."

"No," said Sam after a pause. "No, no. She probably still likes you but is just waiting for you to make a big gesture. There's no way she turned it off that quickly. Invite her to—" Sam was retreating to his car while shaking his head. "—I don't know, a movie?" He slid safely into the Accord and lowered the window.

"A movie? That's your grand gesture?"

"I don't know—we need to formulate plans for getting these girls, that's all. I—I need to think. There's simply got to be something we're overlooking, some missed signal to analyze. We'll talk about this more and figure out why we're losing to these freaking morons. We'll solve this!"

"Goodnight, Sam."

* * *

Benson's F150, soapy-white except for the tarry streaks of mosquito pulp along the hood, barreled down I-35 effortlessly for most of the three-hour drive. Around Round Rock, however, the fellow drivers multiplied and began buzzing about the interstate like hornets. This worsened around Pflugerville, and as it did Max noticed Benson's knuckles whiten around the steering wheel. When he removed a hand from his rigid 10-2 position it was to stab an index finger at the "Track" arrow of the CD player. As the downtown buildings sprang up nearly in unison on the west side of the highway and the first signs appeared for the 12th Street exit to the Texas State Capitol, the traffic clunked to a complete stop. Max remembered from Texas history class that the state capitol building had been designed in a type of Renaissance Revival architecture to mimic the neo-classical stylings of the United States capitol. Everything in America seemed to be a revival of some older generation hopelessly displaced across an ocean and time.

The cessation of highway speeds seemed to pacify Benson enough for Max to ask, "Hey, didn't Sam suggest we take the MoPac to avoid traffic?"

"I'm not taking Sam's advice on much of anything, especially driving." By this, he was alluding to an incident during the summer after freshman year when they were all back in Martha together heading out one night and Sam silently ignored a "Yield" sign and scraped up against an exiting vehicle—which just so happened to be a police cruiser, further contributing to the notoriety of the incident.

"Speaking of Sam," Benson began in a lower tone while cocking his head away from the road for the first time in miles. "Travis says he's different these days. Like, he drinks now, that kind of thing."

"Ben, I can't describe it. He's the old Sam—good Puritanical work ethic, quiet scientific mind and all— but he's different too. The words elude me."

"So is it true? That he drinks now? I don't mean to press the issue like some kind of lush, but this will be a lot more enjoyable trip if Sam's hitting the bottle."

"I don't know, really. We talk on the phone a lot still and email some, but I really haven't seen too much of him in the last year. I can't believe he's drinking now. Remember the way he used to recoil at even the sight of a beer can?"

"I don't know, man. Travis says he's seen Stanley

and him and all that crew closing down bars on Sixth Street."

"Please, I place zero faith in Travis's alleged accounts. If Stanley can sweet talk Sam into getting hammered, then he's a better man than I." Not having seen Stanley and his friends since high school, Max still pictured him as the apish starting center of the basketball team—the type of guy whose family money made him soft with a stooping neck and rounded shoulders, but blessed with an alpha-male exomorphic frame that insulated him from retaliation no matter how careless the verbal misstep. A couple notches up on the high school food chain, he was friendly to Max and his cohorts but generally kept them on the periphery.

"Oh, I almost forgot the best part!" Benson lifted one hand from the steering wheel and suspended an index finger in midair—a lecturer delivering the crux of a diatribe before dismissing class for the weekend. "Travis also claims that Sam has equations or proofs or—I don't know, some bullshit like that—to disprove the existence of God. Have you heard about *that* shit?

"Jesus, whatever. Nothing ever makes any sense with that guy." They laughed.

Benson was double checking the exit sign for Riverside and whisked away Max's incredulity with a garbled mumble while tilting the bulky white Ford off the highway. Max poked around at the concept of God as a mathematical theorem and couldn't see it. Not only was his mind ill-fitted for such computational discourse, but also it seemed like a false hermeneutical question to him—especially odd given the alleged asker. In high school Sam had often (but not too often) suggested his family's church services to Max. These pronouncements were received less as invitations and more like conclusions—the synthesis of a series of unstated premises.

As the paradox of eradicating faith in order to validate it ricocheted around within his skull, they pulled up in front of the beige door near the heart of a sprawling apartment complex. Sam, in mesh athletic shorts, Adidas shoes, and a shrunken gray t-shirt, stood flapping his arms and shouting something that neither driver nor passenger understood.

"Fuckity fuck!" Sam made a rolling motion with a fist, to which Benson complied by arrowing down the automatic window. Up close the shrunken shirt appeared normally proportioned, and instead it was Sam who had been distorted. He had obviously made a point for the first time in his life of hitting the gym, sporting inflated triceps and pecs—all the vanity muscles. At the moment he was slick from sweat and panting like an anxious mutt.

"Stanley locked the door. I don't have a key anymore. He's passed out drunk and not answering the phone. Moron!" This last part came out as an explanation for all the missing context and omission of syntax.

"The fuck are you talking about! Lose your key?" Benson jerked the shift stick into park.

"He's passed out drunk, Stanley is, and he won't wake up to get the door or even answer the phone. They floated the river this afternoon." He slammed down this last fact as if it were accepted science that the Guadalupe River sapped men of consciousness.

"The key, where's your fucking key?" said Benson whose natural complexion nearly resembled a magnolia but had seemingly reddened beneath the sun after only a momentary exposure.

"Well, the thing is—regarding the matter of the key—I don't have one. I mean I did but now I don't—because I don't live here anymore."

"Jesus, Sam, is this a fucking joke?" He turned toward Max, searching for confirmation, but found him absent, having crawled out of the truck and now standing behind Sam peering fruitlessly at the tiny cracks between the gray blinds and the window frame.

Benson too exited the truck and the three high school conspirators stood in wordless conference for a few moments. Then, still silently, Sam walked back to the front of the porch where he seized a package addressed to Stanley Stankowsky. Flanked by Max he schlepped over to the complex's pool and dropped it into the water. The two felt a sprinkle to their faces from the splash, like water from a font.

"What was in the package?" asked Max.

"I'm doing him a favor."

And so, the three of them cast off in Sam's Accord, Max beside him in the stern and Benson in the back. As it turned out, Sam's overnight bag had already been packed and stuffed into his trunk—conveniently, the others remarked—which afforded them the opportunity to set sail under cover of night rather than delaying until Friday morning. The low hum of the dark pavement soon lulled Max to sleep.

The governor could find no favorable corollary to the expanse of rushing water before him, it easily surpassing in ferocity and volume the Ebro or Guadalquivir of his country and certainly the Caquinampo of this hostile world. Squinting his eyes at

*the swirling sting of fresh and saltwater, he liberated
the pockmarked morion from his head, handing it to
Hernandarias de Saavedra, kin to the Marshal of
Seville. Everything across these gulf plains seemed to
Governor Hernando de Soto unrestrained, wrought
with devilish immensity, like the monstrous stature of
the traitorous Chief Tuskaloosa. They had been tested
by the death of his nephew at Atahachi and then led to a
firestorm at Mabila that killed dozens of Spanish
Christians and countless animals. Still, the governor
considered the crossing of this mighty river the most
harrowing challenge yet, and when they succeeded,
nearly unscathed, breaking a native barricade and
weathering a hailstorm of arrows to reach the outer
bank, he considered it a product of divine providence.
Soon thereafter, God manifested his grace through the
native lord of Casqui, who was so moved by the
venerable spirit within Hernando de Soto that he
willfully offered the virginal flesh of his young daughter
to the great Christian commander.*

Max awoke with a start, quickly wresting his mind
from a particularly vivid dream based on an American
history class that he and Benson had taken together at
Atena State and for which they had collaborated on a
presentation rooted in primary source accounts of the
conquistadors. So random to conjure that up now, he
thought.

Despite evading the smoggy heart of Houston's
rush hour, they still encountered the usual slowdowns
on I-10 that seemed to materialize at random even in
patches of the city where traffic was sparse—the great
international port being divorced from zoning so that a
mad developer could plop down a skyscraper or a strip

club wherever he damn well pleased. Just as suddenly as the highway tightened around them, it released them again to plunge onward in the night. The last bit of Texas traffic was a lane closure outside of Beaumont beside a glowing oil refinery that blinked like an airway landing strip and emitted into the air a rubbery and gently caustic odor similar to crazy glue. Even this roadwork that bottle-necked drivers within a narrow passage of orange cones only lasted long enough to draw epithets from each of the three before the highway cleared and sent them unfettered toward the Sabine River and a sign that read, "Bienvenue en Louisianne."

Soon thereafter, the difference in foliage caught up with the separation designated by the manmade boundary—oak trees and orange cups of honeysuckle giving way to tupelo and violet wisteria that partitioned vast boggy fields of emerald that somehow still glowed in the night. The whole landscape of southern Louisiana was mystical, raw, and utterly alien to the boys, despite hailing from a neighboring state (and Sam having mysteriously visited only a week earlier). Every bulb of light that dotted the swamps off past the interstate illuminated an exotic world—humidity hanging in the air as tangibly as wet towels on a clothesline, tiny brick structures that somehow contained both convenience stores and casinos, and an endless blackness to the night sky that draped the terrain in velvet, pressing down upon the soil and towns with the weight of life. To Texans, Louisiana only seemed vaguely southern—an alternate dimension of Mississippi or Arkansas with plantations of sugar instead of cotton, primordial reptiles in place of docile cattle, red-toothed nutria rather than scurrying field mice.

And then, the scattered points of light coalesced into a city: Lafayette. Even highway exit signs here revealed a history that diverged from that of the deep south with French words and names of saints. Just east of Lafayette, and still nestled deeply into Acadiana, was the town of Breaux Bridge, which declared itself to be the "World Capitol of Crawfish" via painted signs. A short jog off the interstate was a Cajun seafood diner operating out of a log cabin. Across the road and down a couple football fields in length was a freshly paved shopping center hosting a Super Target as its crown jewel. Benson and Max were placing hyperbolic bets with Sam that the restaurant wouldn't be open at nearly midnight in a "random shithole town"—Benson's wording. As Sam well knew, they were in fact open until 2:00—all night on weekends. In Texas, they could never find a decent meal after 10:00 pm.

Sam thumbed through the oversized, laminated menu and nearly gagged at the picture of crawfish in a bucket. The red little crustaceans resembled cockroaches to him, and having a phobia of insects, he safely ordered a burger with American-style yellow cheese. Benson and Max each ordered a bowl of crawfish etouffee, which Benson considered a "fucking rip-off" at $10 a plate. He whispered his diagnosis to both of his tablemates while thrusting an index finger at Sam. Max, thumbing through some crumpled bills in his pocket, voiced no such protestations, silently devouring the creamy white rice dampened by a pink roux sauce.

He couldn't have described to his co-conspirators, had he the inclination to do so, the faraway feeling welling inside him. He hadn't traveled outside of Texas since being dragged across the country in a van as a teenager. When he left Martha for college at Atena State, the drive was less than an hour, and any symbolism of the move away from home felt hollowed out. When his mom offered a rare cliché, it was "Well, today is the first day of the rest of your life." And then she turned and left to join his father, who was waiting below in a running car out front of the midrise dormitory. She paused momentarily, which he suspected was meant for reflection, before slipping wordlessly into the night. Max unpacked the clothes that his mother had washed and ironed the day before. After neatly sliding around his new luggage and an old backpack across his half of a gray concrete floor, he wandered down the hall to find Benson, who had already arranged for them to meet with some other high school chums down in the Bowie Hall lobby.

There in Breaux Bridge, however, chewing the unctuous stringiness of the crawfish—a tiny creature whose shriveled stature belied its rich flavor, which was imbued with the earthy minerals of vast seas—he felt for the first time in his adult life a shapeless tomorrow that he could pluck from the pregnant blackness of the night.

They divvied the check three ways and took turns in the restroom. The final shift belonged to Benson, and while he was away from the table, Sam remarked, "I have to sleep as much as possible before we get to New Orleans. You're going to have to drive." He glanced off toward the restroom and then at his wristwatch. "God damn, it's late. You're going to have to push the pace a bit because we are well behind schedule."

"Sure, but why me? Why can't Ben's ass drive?"

"He's too—he just won't." They both nodded in conspiratorial alignment. "And he would be too careful on the highway. It would take us for fucking ever to get there—so late we wouldn't be able to go out tonight."

"And what's with you being so reckless, hotshot? Usually you're the cautious one. Or, used to be." Benson sidled up wordlessly behind them, and with a half glance back at him, Sam began leading Max out of the neon glow of the restaurant and into the enveloping blackness as Benson, who was fumbling with his new cellular phone, trailed some distance behind. His mother had bought him the phone out of judicious maternal purview, and it was she who was presently calling. Benson weighed obligation against common sense before answering. He hated talking on the phone in public, and given the time of night, he calculated that his mother was likely finishing off a bottle of Beaujolais by then.

While issuing the third mumbled approbation for whatever drunken advice his mother tossed through the phone at him, the others climbed into the front of the Accord, reversing spots.

"OK, what the hell is up with you lately?" asked Max.

Sam craned his neck toward the backseat that was vacantly awaiting the violent thrust of a door. The car was spotless everywhere but the driver's seat, which had faded from a verdant green into more of a pea soup and sported a brown stain in the shape of a Maltese cross.

"No, what do you mean? OK, look—I'll tell you later." And with that Sam flicked his head again toward the backseat just before Benson popped in and packed

away his phone—not into a pocket but actually put
away within an overnight bag.

They slid onward down the velvety pavement
through cryptic corners of Louisiana bayou that were
only half revealed by the deceptive glow of the
interstate. Lulled to sleep like a colicky baby in the
backseat, Benson had checked out of their spotty
conversation: an oral reunion of bringing up so-and-so
who hadn't quite been forgotten but never cut deep
enough into their lives to bother with, outside of breezy
boredom. Seeing Sam slump toward the window, Max
pounced.

"Sam, what was in the boxes—the ones you threw
in the pool."

"Books."

"And did those books harm you in some way?
Stanley doesn't exactly strike me as the reading type.
Why not bust up his tires or hell, I don't know, grab a
credit card application from the mailbox and fill it out
in his name—something a sane person would do."

"No. Jesus, no! What's wrong with you? I wasn't
trying to dick him over. I mean I was, but not really. I
was doing him a favor, if you must know."

"Didn't look like it."

"His girlfriend ordered them from this church in
Desoto that her family goes to. They're a series about
how young men and women can find proof of the lord
through everyday life. It's dangerous."

"And what about you? Are you no longer seeing
proof of the lord? Has the pious Goodman Eaglin
strayed from the flock?"

"You know that famous quote by Saint
Augustine?"

"No."

"Yeah, you do, everyone does. About asking God for salvation, but not yet."

"OK, sure I've heard that before."

"Well, that's bullshit. It's easy. Anyone can live an epicurean youth and then seek redemption once you've settled into middle age and have a wife and family or what have you. It's the inverse that's mind-numbing, soul crushing. Do you get my meaning?" He didn't wait for a response. "You don't. So, I wanted to study physics because I thought I could get to know the Hawkings and Bohrs and Maxwells and see where their humanistic bullshit politics clouded their ability to—I guess see proof of the sublime spiritual world. And, the further I got the more it seemed like the geniuses of the modern world were, indeed, geniuses and that there was going to be no disproving them."

"Shit, you sure did turn on a dime."

"Not really. It was the last couple of years of hanging out with Stanley and those guys and feeling how out of tune and—what's the word—unfounded all my bullshit Sunday school assumptions of life were."

"So it's true then. You discovered equations?"

"Equations? Huh?"

"Forget it. Nothing."

For several minutes they slinked on in silence, piercing the boggy darkness with their twin orbs of glowing halogen. And then: brake lights up ahead. Sitting nakedly alone atop the Atchafalaya Swamp's raw underbelly, Sam's Toyota suddenly found itself stashed within a community of red brake lights.

They slowed.

Benson cursed and spit something out the window.

They slowed more.

Sam and Max cursed too, though Sam's curse came out more as a bestial howl or grunt, and for a moment Max thought his friend might actually be in some kind of physical pain.

The truth revealed itself.

The interstate traffic had ceased altogether—and, though formerly spaced out across dozens of miles of dark pavement, countless strangers were now flung together, collectively illuminating the black highway as a shantytown of muttering disappointment. Pretty soon the three of them noticed figures floating about and brake lights downgraded to parking lights—and then blinked into oblivion.

They too shut off their engine, and Max was the first to emerge from the car. He wanted a cigarette. It wasn't that he couldn't have waited under conventional circumstances, but it just seemed like something a 60s tough guy would have done in the movies. He wasn't entirely sure what decade he was stepping into, but he was pretty sure 2002 wasn't a part of any. The aughts— what sort of name was that? How does that stack up against the 20s? the 50s? Those had men in double-breasted suits at train stations or sporting ice cream colors for summer flirtations at the Harvard Club with some dainty beauty speaking in an affected non-rhotic accent and wearing satin gloves—as if the world at large were too grimy for the delicate whiteness of her hands.

Benson made small talk with a trucker while Max and Sam peered over the bridge's safety rail at the black swamp below. The night air was dewy and sweetly foreboding. Something rippled within the still water below and they pictured an alligator submerging its nostrils to prepare an assault.

"OK, fancy boys, I'm going back to the car to rest my eyes." Benson had snuck up behind them. "The dude I was talking to heard over his CB there was a major wreck a few miles ahead, and the highway's shut down for an investigation. No telling how long that'll be—what with the swamp on either side." Something splashed below.

"Somebody better be fucking dead," snarled Sam.

"Jesus, that's a hell of a thing to say, Sam. Somebody probably is dead if they're shutting the whole damn road down. The trucker said they have to search through debris even down in the mucky water. A car was apparently off on the shoulder, what little there is of one, changing a tire when an 18-wheeler swerved just a little and hit him."

"I didn't mean I want someone to be dead. I just meant there should be a justification or—Christ, it sounds bad in context, I admit."

"Whatever, I'll see you guys back in the car." As Benson left, Max stamped out the burning cherry of his cigarette on the pavement, then scraped the ashy evidence from his sole onto the stiff guardrail.

"Shit, you know what I meant, right?" Max nodded and somehow felt that he did understand, tinged with empathy even. What he wanted to ask Sam, however, was why this delay shook him up so badly. At the moment he was fixated by a girl in cutoffs, who had climbed out of the passenger seat and up atop the car, singing some incoherent popish slush and swaying her hips in a grinding motion until her boyfriend or whomever coaxed her to hop down into his arms and back to earth. Sam cocked his head like a retriever desperately wishing to please his master but uncomprehending the command. Rather than attraction to the girl, Sam's gaze seemed to Max more like a museum patron studying a new exhibit. In the daylight it would have been unnerving.

"Ha!" A thought that had been germinating in Max's head suddenly sprouted. "If Ben hadn't taken a piss before we left the restaurant, we could have been right in the middle of that accident. Maybe even dead." He was only slightly embarrassed at his own excitement.

"Life is random." Sam said it as if it were the last line of a terrible novel—a *deus ex machina* at the peak of an emotional ascent. Nonetheless, it was indeed the final word as they retreated back to the Toyota and resigned themselves to sleep.

* * *

A horn blared from behind in a sustained note—the type that follows a series of unheeded staccato warnings—accompanied by a rhythmic pulsation of bright lights.

"What's happening?" Max, behind the wheel, snapped his head up and squinted into the rearview mirror.

"Go, we're going!" said Sam.

"Huh, only an hour," remarked Benson.

Cars streamed past them on the right as Max brought the engine to life and caught up to highway speed.

"You can speed up," said Sam. "No one's getting

pulled over tonight."

* * *

Lake Pontchartrain, massive, inky as a starless constellation, lay in wait before them, a final warning beyond which but eternally flowing inland were indifferent gulf waters that spit back onto land the unrepentant pools that the Mississippi expelled. The bridge yawned beneath the night crawlers, stretching out as a burning caterpillar. Max knew that something ancient and musty—the mined core of hominid experience awaited him on the other side.

Sam, who had urgently commandeered his own car moments earlier, exited toward the Superdome and, employing a deftness unknown to the others, navigated the side streets of the Garden District and into Downtown and then the French Quarter, eventually pushing his way down Carondelet toward Canal. The directions, printout out via MapQuest, lay inert and neatly folded within Benson's luggage. At the intersection with Canal, Carondelet became Bourbon and right on cue a brass band uniformed in conical hats came swaying outward with the bells of their horns rapidly oscillating from one side of the street to the other. A solitary tenor sax player marooned on the sidewalk beside an open black case of dollar bills momentarily dipped the mouthpiece to his breast and succumbed to the rolling wave of sound. A woman in her mid-forties, tanned into a shriveled shell of a body, danced just a few steps ahead of the procession with a fluid swirl that somehow complemented her sinewy torso—occasionally kicking aside plastic beads and cups without breaking her rhythm. Up to the right a group of frat boys, some sporting their Greek letters on pastel t-shirts, stomped out of Krystal Burger with grease-stained white bags of food. The tallest among them cupped both hands to his mouth and began yelling, "Fuck you! Fuck all of you!" His friends finally intervened as he hoisted a burger in the air and prepared to launch it at a trombone. At that point Max switched off the car radio, which had been tuned to a local zydeco station with jangly percussion and an accordion-led melody that seemed to jump all over the speakers, and cracked the window. The dancing woman locked eyes with Sam long enough to smile and mouth something that could have been "Good luck" just before she stuck a two-foot hop over a beige hill of vomit near the curb.

"Heya, Sam, I don't think this is the right Holiday Inn. This one here with the big clarinet mural is on Bourbon and ours is supposed to be on Royal," called Benson from the backseat.

"Well, ours is supposed to be in the French Quarter. This is the French Quarter."

"Dude, this isn't what the map says to do. We're a few blocks away."

"Just, how about you go in and talk to them, Ben, while we park the car. I have my cell phone turned on in case you need to call." Sam had pulled over in front of the hotel while throngs of shouting, sticky tourists passed by in either direction only a few feet from the car. Benson shook his head but played along, as Sam stared down Bourbon, regarding the scene with the desperate hope of a combat soldier returning to an unfaithful lover. The slam of the car door on one side by Benson was echoed on the other when some meaty hand slapped down on the hood of the car to alert its inhabitants of a girl jumping in the middle of the street with her top proudly lifted to her neck. Her smile only eroded when a balled-up clump of beads whacked her on the cheek, halting her pogo-stick-like bouncing and forcing her to stretch her sweat-soaked floral blouse back over her exposed, pendulous breasts—to which onlookers of all sexes hooted and shrieked.

"OK, while Ben's busy confirming that we're at the wrong hotel, we'll have some time to talk," began Sam.

"You bastard."

"Whatever, he'll figure it out and walk a couple blocks to Royal—probably go to bed at that point—doesn't matter. We don't have much time, have to get to Bourbon Street Blues before 3:00 and it's nearly 2:30 already. We may be too late even so. Listen, I have to tell you about Electra."

"Jesus. Yes, talk if you have a story to tell. You seem to be full of ulterior motives—" Max trailed off as he watched Sam's phone light up with the words "Ben Cell." Sam snatched it up with a sigh.

"OK, hello?—Yeah, my bad I guess. So, ah, how about you just walk over there and check in while we park. We'll meet at Bourbon Street Blues when you get out." Max noticed that Sam had halted on a secluded side street and was backing into a narrow gap between cars. The road was illuminated only by the distant pale green of a hospital parking garage. "I promise that it's only like two blocks. You can walk it, man. Two freaking blocks."

Bourbon Street Blues Company was neither a blues

house nor much of a company. The cover band on stage alternated between 80s power ballads like "Sweet Child of Mine" and thumping punk-pop. The 30-something vocalist wore knee-high red leather boots and a black spandex top that snapped up against her perspiring torso. She writhed and flashed her teeth at the dancefloor comprised of a couple dozen groping men, a giant bachelorette party in matching custom t-shirts (a sequined silhouette of the gaping-mouthed bride confronted by a comically shaped dildo), and a side dish of meaty locals who danced the most aggressively and least purposefully. The singer began hopping up and down, evenly shifting directions and yelping into the microphone. Her voice, a sort of crème brulée of sugary ease immolated into a rough-textured coating when she began, then switched to that of a harpy as she shrieked at the crowd to "Get up!"

A slap stung Max across the shoulder blade. He swiveled around, half-expecting a fist from a peeved local, only to see Sam's face, wide-eyed, sucking at the caustic air. He looked as if he'd been running wind sprints and taking shots. As it turns out, that wasn't far off.

"Electra's still here—but she's not a shot girl anymore. She's bartending upstairs." He gulped from a giant plastic cup between violent respirations. "I told you about her, right?"

"Not really."

"OK, well there's not time for a diatribe now, but I met her when I was in town with Stanley and that crew. Just a week ago she was one of those girls walking around with trays full of test tube shots. Now she's a bartender upstairs."

"Cool, and—so what about her? She hot or something?"

"Yeah, I guess. I mean she has a certain look—that I like."

"And should I assume that something happened between you two a week ago?"

"I mean yeah, sure. Not like anything official, but there was definitely something there. You'll see, but we gotta catch her upstairs. I'll tell you more later."

"I can't even tell if you answered my question."

Upstairs was almost as congested as the main bar but quieter with bouncy pop pulsing through the speakers in lieu of live music. The black-painted wooden stairway was too narrow to truly accommodate the alternate flow of traffic, but the revelers made it work. The guys carefully contorted themselves to avoid contact with one another while the girls freely swayed their sweaty bodies and rubbed, catlike, up against strangers. A short, pudgy girl with dark curls and naked arms pawed at random men for balance as she navigated her descent. "Smile," she said to Sam before anointing both him and Max with beads. People were always telling Sam to smile.

"What does that even mean?" He genuinely wanted to know, but just as Max reached for an answer, Sam waved him off.

"Hold on!" He swung his arms like a traffic cop. "We can't just walk up to the bar. We need a plan."

"A plan? My plan is to order a drink at the bar— from the bartender." Max tilted his beer bottle upward, then tossed it in the trash—the clang of glass barely registering above the frenzy of the crowd. Sam sidestepped Max, eclipsing him from a direct view of the bar across the room. Nevertheless, he craned his neck around the taller man, seeing only a hapless barback and a wall of frat boys in polos. A dark thought swirled around the scummy waters of his mind, but before he could mouth the words "she doesn't exist" a petite blond laminated by a brilliant royal blue halter top (the recognizable BBC uniform) backed into him to evade a groping middle-aged man in a blazer with a red, moistened face. She crunched down on his foot in the process. Instead of apologizing (girls never seemed to in these places) she swung around with her tray of glass tubes and simply said, "Shots?"

"Yes! For him, he needs them." Sam's eyes, previously bestial, were now focused. He never bought rounds.

The shots were cartoonish—bright blue and red and yellow—the type of thing that belonged in a witch's cauldron from a fairy tale or an overzealous production of *Macbeth*. Max reached out his hand, but Sam smacked it away. "No, man, not like that." Suddenly he was a beatnik. Instead of handing the drinks over, the girl—Anastasia, according to her name tag (if you could ever trust those things)—slid the bottom of two test tubes into her knowing mouth and then squeezed the back of his neck. Then with surprising athleticism, she forced him down and rose to her tiptoes above him, flipping the glass tubes upside down and spilling syrupy liquor down his throat. She wiped her lips with a bony hand, snatched cash from Sam and jammed it down her black apron—performing her work with unflappable focus, even holding a steady gaze as two, three, then four swollen bouncers materialized out of nowhere (seemingly forged out of nickel and cadmium from the very riven-flavored air surrounding them) to snuff out an escalating shoving match between college boys.

They chatted: Anastasia with the angular downturn of a trochaic Slavic voice, Sam wildly gesturing and limning sideways peeks at the bar, and Max with a growing warmth that stretched from his loins into his breast. She departed and others took her place—black, white, brown—some with non-rhotic Cajun accents that would have resembled raspy versions of a coastal New England dialect, if they hadn't been roughened by southern poverty. Eventually the guys tired of being dipped by the shot girls and just grabbed the glasses. By 4:00 am they were buying as much alcohol for the shot girls as for themselves. The girls, some feigning visceral enthusiasm and others not bothering, all accepted, knowing they couldn't end their shifts until the trays were empty. It was true too that the shots were more akin to a vat of Mrs. Butterworth's than real liquor. Glycemic index be damned, Max thought, which sent him into wondering what these young women were indexing at home. Cash? Sure, but there was something else. He tried vainly to consider their home lives. Did they traipse across the French Quarter, past Canal, and into suburban places like Metairie or Kenner with the same smiling bravado? Impossible. They were specters fated to restlessly float about these haunts for eons—in his mind.

Sam disappeared for a few minutes, which would have gone unnoticed by Max, as Anastasia had returned during her rounds, and the two were discussing dirty words in Russian and finishing off the last two shots of her shift. He felt a ballooning insistence in his stomach that tickled his esophagus and cautioned him against any more greedy gulps. Instead he sipped delicately from the test tube and hoped his pale flush was dimmed by the dull orange bulbs.

"One more you have." It wasn't a question exactly. She raised the lonely shot to her lips and, apparently forgetting they had evolved past the ritual several conversational stages ago, dipped the elongated glass into her mouth and then began swaying her hips to the smoothly thumping bass of Big Tymers' "Still Fly." Max recognized the song from the Dallas rap station way up at the top of the FM dial, but the bar staff—all of them erupting into a dance—knew the group as homegrown locals. Anastasia's dancing was daintier, almost a modified cha-cha, by contrast to the NOLA natives who stabbed their hips aggressively with an atavistic urgency. She slid the tube back into her mouth, this time punctuating the depth she achieved by rolling her eyes back into her head. Max's stomach felt pinched off and he searched for the words that could halt her advance but, finding non, braced for the cold burning liquor to be ejected down his throat as she rose above him and shoved him down by the shoulders.

Max paid and tipped her, barely noting through the haze of exhilarating sickness that he'd spent nearly all his money on the first night.

"Where'd she go? Hey, hey, get her back here!" Sam had plied his way through a thinning crowd and now stood, apish, either nervously or drunkenly shifting his weight back and forth.

"Who, the shot girl?"

"Yeah, yes get her back here. I mean you were progressing with her, right?"

"I guess we were talking for a while. She sold out her tray and went to change out of her apron. Said she'd come back, but whatever."

"She said that? Said she'd be back? Those exact words?"

"Jesus yes, but I'm not holding my breath. Besides—listen—um, I gotta go puke."

"No, no! Gotta wait here for her. Said she'd be back so you wait. You wait for her like she's fucking Odysseus!" Definitely drunk, Max concluded, satisfied that they were on the same frequency.

The men's room upstairs consisted of a piss trough and a door-less toilet stall, which is where Max purged restless acids from his gut. There were already pink chunks sliding down the graffitied black walls from a previous occupant, and the bitter scent aided in the expediency of his own evacuation. A couple frat guys who had come in to piss cheered him on as if her were a pole dancer who'd finally gotten naked.

* * *

Ben stepped out of the shower with the bleached white towel folded divinely around his pale waist. He glowered down pityingly at the mass of humanity who apparently shared the other queen bed. He mumbled something at Sam that evoked only a guttural grunt—or perhaps it was a cough? Max attempted wanly to put back into his mind the past few hours. As far as he could reconstruct the final moments of the night, it was if he stepped out of BBC and into a wormhole that transported him (with a violent assault to his skull) into the bed, an offering to the vengeful morning light.

"Nothing good," Sam murmured in apparent response to some interrogative. Having abruptly lost interest in this line of questioning, Benson addressed the question of their morning. Filling the daylight hadn't been seriously pondered by any of them, as the day constituted in their young imaginations little more than a convalescent period between nocturnal bouts.

"Get up, assholes." Benson was now jamming feet into tennis shoes and reading the instruction on the coffee machine. "We gotta go get those beignets. That's what people do in this swampy hell; talked to some old man in the lobby last night while you two fun boys were out getting ripped off by shot girls. Sam, look up Café du Monde in the phone book and call for directions. Ask if we can walk. Max, you gonna puke again? Do your business, pop an aspirin or whatever, and get the hell up."

They shoved their way through the revolving door and out into the brutal August sun that seared their eyes and sent ripples of pain through their minds that had been wrung dry, except for Ben, who bounced from step to step, lording his physical prowess over the other two. The heat blanketed them like the hug of a cranky, corpulent uncle, but it differed from the Texas sun. Instead of waves of baking heat, the Louisiana sky felt like a slap upside the head by a warm, soapy sponge. They worked their way back down Bourbon Street, away from Canal and toward the downriver thrust of the Mississippi. The whole theatre of the French Quarter was animated by the late morning light, as Max could hardly reconcile his final sputtering memories of the previous night, which included bruised knees on pavement, thunderous street sweepers like angels of

God cleansing the wicked, greasy bites of food from Krystal Burger, and primal shouts—likely at no one in particular. Today the street had come to life and danced shirtless, baring glassy caramel flesh, animated by spouts of sweat. The stinging earthiness of burning maduro-wrapped cigars floated after them out of shops and slithered down the sidewalk. A second line danced and swayed past them down the center of the road, trombones jutting their brass bells outward into golden erections. They crossed Iberville and Bienville (streets named for the city fathers) and then Conti, which was the relic of the royal house of Bourbon, now adorned by Spanish architecture and mongrelized shotgun domiciles. Finally they reached the corner of Bourbon and St. Louis where Sam and Max barely recognized BBC from the previous night. It was wide open. It never closed. But in the daylight with the wide doors flung open to welcome families of tourists in from the street, it seemed domesticated, a kitschy emptiness with gray concrete floors and clownish carnival barkers hoisting oversized cardboard signs trying to reel in yawning passersby. Down St. Louis, marching away from Bourbon, they passed museums, art galleries, upscale hotels, a voodoo shop with a sacred altar (just past the tarot cards and Haitian straw hoodoo dolls), and a coffee roaster that marinated the entire intersection in a glaze of cedar, cacao, and even a zesty sweetness like bergamot. Here they turned left and followed Decatur to Jackson Square, flanked by tourist trap bar and grills on one side and the St. Louis Cathedral on the other. A trickle of other pedestrians clogged up into a sweaty mess of humanity, along with bikes and cars and even a horse-drawn carriage, which irked a honking middle-aged local in thick-rimmed glasses. They were at the right place, Café du Monde, as evidenced by the powdery white streaks of sugar that punctuated the sidewalk like lines of cocaine.

They ate beignets, drank café au lait and then wandered past the sidewalk musicians and painted street performers and through the shops of Jackson Square and eventually to the narrow mall by the river where they blended in with the general flow of foot traffic and exchanged smiles with families of fellow customers. The workers, darker and more confident than their Bourbon Street counterparts, bagged trinkets and slid change back more slowly and with narrower eyes than the bartenders and shot girls from the previous night.

Benson excused himself to shop for something—penny loafers, Saint Lauren wallet? Who knows what he actually told them. Left in possession of Ben's phone, Max recognized the number that popped up on the screen and answered after three or four rings.

"Hi, Jess," he began tentatively. He watched as Sam wandered off back toward the mall's downriver exit.

"Hi, baby. You—you never called me back yesterday. I thought you were gonna say goodnight?"

"Oh, yeah, sorry, I guess I fell asleep. Listen, there's so much good food here, and I keep thinking about how much you'd love it. Maybe I could come back with you? We'd have so much fun, Jess."

"Oh my God, really? I'd love that! We never go out of town—together anyway. When should we go? Should we go before or after San Antonio?

"Well, I don't know. We'll figure all that out later

on. But listen, what are you doing today? I miss you!"
He meant it too, at least for the time it took to say the
words. Who knew what feeling would pour over him
when basking under the mystical, moist air of the New
Orleans night.

"Oh my God, the wedding was so beautiful, even
though it was hot and—"

"Yeah, I was just about to ask about that—your
cousin, right?"

"You totally forgot I was going to it, didn't you?
Until I said something just now."

"No, that's not—no, I was just about to ask you
about it. I just meant about tonight."

"Tamara wants me to come over to her house and
hangout with them, so I guess I'll go. I mean, it's not
like I have anything else to do with you gone." Max
wished Sam hadn't disappeared. Standing there holding
Ben's phone, alone in a strange city, he felt naked—a
tourist stripped of that outward veneer of ease and
indulgence.

"Who's 'them'? Let me guess: it's not just going to
be you and Tamara."

"Don't do that. It's just going to be Tamara and—
and Slade, OK? What's the big deal?"

"Of course that dude has to be there. And—and
even after what's happened in the past, you're probably
going to get drunk with him tonight, aren't you?"

"And you're not going to get drunk tonight?"

"Listen, I have to go find Sam." With that, he hung
up and stomped off toward the exit. He didn't realize
when he first started off that he already knew where he
was going. That is, he knew where Sam had gone.

* * *

That night, as Sam showered, Ben and Max slumped on separate beds. While Ben thumbed lazily on the remote control, pausing at each movie only until he could identify the cast, Max twisted his neck into a hapless knot to spy around the flesh-colored cantilever that obscured his view of the pedestrians below on Royal.

"Jake Gyllenhaal—douche."

"You should see the people out here. These girls, where do they come from? It's like a different species." Max stood up for a better look. "Little jean shorts and pig tails and cheap beads they wouldn't touch back home. Why is he a douche?"

"I don't know, just is. I've got nothing against him really. He never shaves is the thing. In interviews he's always got some trendy stubble like he doesn't care, but he cares enough to look like he doesn't care as his trademark." He flipped the channel.

"They pick this shit off the sticky street like it's Betsey Johnson or whatever it is girls like now, and they just drape themselves in it like it's nothing. If some sap in any other city in America snatched up a piece of plastic trash from the stinking street, then offered it to his woman—AND demanded that she first take off her top—she would slap him or run. Fight or flight. Either way it would be perceived as a horrific threat. Who's the elf chick?"

"Who, Galadriel? You joking? That's Cate Blanchett all trying to pretend she's not Australian." Symphonic cellos swelled to a legato crescendo in the background. "Nah, she's good I guess. She was in *The*

Talented Mr. Ripley with Matt Damon. Good movie but don't get me started on that guy."

Max draped back onto the bed and, lowering his voice, offered, "So, I asked him about the 'God equations.'"

"Jesus, that's so fucking stupid. Of course he didn't actually come up with equations to disprove God. Travis Kim's just dramatic is all."

"Yeah, sure, I realize that. But I wanted to see his reaction. He definitely is not the good Christian soldier any more, that's for sure. He's like—he's like a blind kid swinging at a piñata."

Ben chortled. "What is that supposed to mean? Oh shit, there's Rudy. I mean it's Sean Astin playing a hobbit. Always a diminutive character. Let's see, *Rudy* was from '93, I believe. Eight years later, still playing a short loser. Anyway, you were saying—"

"I was saying it's like he's a blind kid entrusted with a big stick for the first time, and he's whacking it all over the place in a frenzy of pent up energy, but he can't actually hit anything because he's never held a stick or seen a piñata. Since he doesn't know what a pinata looks like, he imagines them everywhere, even in places where they clearly don't exist."

"You guys are getting weird on me. Whatever, he'll figure it out." The splash of the shower sloshed off.

"There's one more thing," said Max, barely above a whisper. I'm not supposed to tell you about this, but he's obsessed with this bartender named Electra."

"Yeah, he's a weirdo, whatever. He meet her the last time he came down here with the Stanley Stankowsky crew?"

"I guess. But no, that's thing about it—I'm not sure she exists."

* * *

Just after midnight at the Old Absinthe House, Benson announced his departure. The three had each ordered an absinthe at the bar and studiously observed as the bartender placed glass goblets, filled them with the earthy spirit, then topped them with perforated, trowel-like silver spoons. Placing a sugar cube on each, he then poured cool water from a decanter that melted down the rigid lines of the crystalline sweetener. The brilliant emerald green liquid in Max's glass grew from a dark monstrous color into a bright, airy bouquet that shone an almost atmospheric glint from the street lantern. Sam motioned for the bartender to pour more water into his glass, thus diluting his rich green into a pale, swampy nothingness. Benson, who sat in a shadow cast by the brick pillar at the bar, sipped from a milky glass that was nearly gray.

"La louche!" said the bartender.

"Tastes like licorice," Ben offered.

"Anise," corrected the bartender, who collected his tips and turned his attention to a group of middle-aged women settling in across from them.

"This is disgusting." Sam drank it anyway in a single gulp. He was checking his watch and eyeing the other two. "Just drink it all at once. It's better that way."

"I don't mind it actually," said Max, sampling greedily.

"Here, finish mine then." Ben slid his glass across

the copper bar top to Max, making the murky, dark cloud of the beverage light up within the ambient bath of the street light. "Can't drink this shit, I'm outta here. You losers enjoy yourselves. Try not to make too much noise with all your ladies when you make it back to the room. Ha!"

This was not unexpected. A few minutes earlier, when Sam had ducked into the bathroom, Ben had said this: "I'm not gonna waste my time over at that same bar again tonight just to watch that idiot embarrass himself sniffing around for some fake chick. Good luck with that shit, son!"

The two who remained noticed the eclectic group of women across them at the bar. One was a plump blond with a cardinal red boa draped over her shoulder. She was the leader—a woman of about 45 with a weighty diamond ring and a pink hue across her cheeks. She swung her arms wildly and sometimes waved her boa to the cackling approval of the others who looked older—or maybe just were soberer. This loud one seemed to loosely direct her gestures at Max and Sam without actually making eye contact, the way a stage performer engages a darkened audience whom she can't quite make out. There was a fourth member of their party who sat a few feet away but laughed enthusiastically enough at the blonde's antics. This other one was younger, less amused and less scandalized by the gesticulations of her friend that cast them as the gravitational center of the quiet bar. All four were in evening dresses, perhaps having come from a play, but this younger one had gauzy patches of her black dress that strategically revealed a taut form. Her eyes, prettier than the delicate baby blues within the puffy casing of her blond friend, were outlined in dramatic strokes of black that eroded the boundary between her tan face and the dark wells of her eyes. While the other three were peacocking at large—really for no one but themselves yet with the convenience of a test group—the younger one sought out, and reached, Max with her searchlight eyes.

"Oh, come on you're not seriously checking out those ladies, are you?" said Sam, noticing this. "They're old. They—whatever. We have to go to BBC. Like now. Electra's about to get off work and I paid dearly for that information."

"Yeah, no, not the old ones," said Max without breaking eye contact. "The one in the back. Do you understand?"

"I don't see her. We gotta go."

"What's wrong with your eyes? How do you not see her—right there!" He motioned with his head.

"Yeah, OK, I see her," he lied. "Doesn't matter, we gotta go."

"Go without me. I'll catch up with you in a few minutes."

"OK, OK, ten minutes." He held up ten fingers for emphasis. "Don't be tardy!"

Seeing Max now alone on the street-lit side of the bar, the girl came over and sat next to him, seemingly unnoticed by her friends. She scrunched her mouth into something resembling a smile and squinted the flesh around her deep eyes that looked like it had been smudged by burnt sage. There was something about her scent—not quite cigarette smoke but rather the burning cinders of a cedar forest set ablaze. Extending a hand, she shook harshly like a man, but as she did this the lacy black hem of her blouse lifted to reveal an elaborate bluish tattoo across a flat, olive stomach—a Balkan skin tone, Max imagined. The figure on her stomach was formless, ghostly within a billowing robe and a tangled wreath of grape vines atop her stacks of curly hair. Dangling from the figure's right hand was the disconsolate face of a tragic mask like a severed head. Jutting from her left hand was a long blade.

"Melpomene," she said suddenly. "You were looking at my tattoo, right? That's me—I mean that's my name, Melpomene."

"The muse of tragedy," said Max dreamily.

"That's right! God, no one gets that. Are you sure you're real? The wormwood does make one hallucinate, and we were both drinking absinthe. Are you my hallucinatory angel, or am I yours?" She leaned back, seemingly pleased with her question, and lit a cigarette.

"I don't know." Dear lord, he thought, she actually wants an answer. She scrutinized him, narrowing her eyes and cogitating on something—not his words exactly but his aura. Max fidgeted under her gaze. Her energy was like the sun's, being simultaneously unbearable and life-affirming.

"What are you thinking about? No, don't tell me, I already know! You're cute, but you're suspicious of strange women who approach you. You're afraid I'm going to lead you astray from your nervous friend who was sitting here and wreck your night."

"Actually, I was thinking about your name. I mean, is it really Melpomene?"

"Maybe it is and I go by 'Mel' for short, or maybe it's something more prosaic like 'Melanie.' Who fucking cares? Hey, listen, let's get out of here. And don't worry, I'll take good care of you and return you safely to your boyfriend soon enough."

They walked slowly down Bourbon, side-stepping coiled beads like shed snakeskin. At one corner, as they waited for agitated cars to whisk away pedestrians while crossing the street, she kissed him. It was firmer than he was used to, and despite being equal to him in height, she cradled his head in her hands as if he were an infant. She repeated such kisses at each pause on their walk and held his hand in between. They were deep kisses that lasted a few seconds at a time, but Max detected something else, an urgency to her.

He told her along the walk about Sam's quest to track down Electra.

"The girls who work on Bourbon are not to be trusted," she said. "They'll tell guys anything to keep them paying. Half of them are part-time prostitutes. Russian hookers especially are everywhere."

"I don't even know if this Electra girl is real. I feel like he's losing his God damned mind."

"I'm sure she's as real as you and I." She laughed.

They stopped at a Wizard of Oz-themed club just past St. Anne, heading downriver. Music thumped from a dark interior, which contrasted with the golden brick outer façade and rainbow frescoes surrounding slim windows. A man in a white t-shirt and grimy jeans came smiling toward them on the sidewalk.

"'Scuse me, ma'am, I was just going to say that's some lovely ink on you. What is that?" He turned to Max. "How're you doing, young man? Say, do either of you have a cigarette you could part with? I've had a long day, and I'm fresh out."

"Naw, take it somewheay else!" A New Orleans

accent broke loose from her for the first time, like the initial crack in a levee.

"These blacks," she said after the man limped away to the dimly lit side of the street "are worse than the hookers."

"Is that fair to—"

"You don't understand," she interrupted. "I'm not saying all blacks, just the ones in the French Quarter. Watch out. They're tricksters who prey on tourists. I've lived in N'awlins my whole life, and I'm not racist or anything, but everyone here knows how it is. Trust me, we know. WE know!"

Please stop talking, Max said to her in his mind. He was already measuring the ethical implications of spending time with a bigot and didn't need to introduce any more evidence. He couldn't quite process at the time what about her declaration of being *not racist* made him so queasy inside. It irked him almost as much as her emphasis on *we*. "So what about your friends at the Old Absinthe House? You didn't need to tell them where you were going?"

"They weren't my friends—just met them tonight." She looked uncomfortable. "Listen, I need you to do a favor for me." She was fishing in her purse for something that momentarily eluded her.

"What's that?" He felt to be sure his moldy-smelling leather wallet was still snuggly lodged into his sweaty back pocket.

"You got any cash? Just a few bucks is enough. I must have left my money at the last bar. I had a twenty." She was still combing through the contents of her purse. "But fuck, I guess it's gone. Listen, babe, I need you to go in there and ask for a bartender named

Hadley; ask him for some pink; he'll know what that means. Pay him whatever you can, twenty bucks would be ideal, but whatever you got is fine."

"What the hell, sure," said Max. He reasoned that as long as he recognized he was being scammed, then that awareness would mitigate the psychic damage. Plus, he only had a ten-dollar bill in his pocket and not much more in his checking account. When you're broke, he concluded, bad ideas bring little risk and proportionally high reward. No wonder so many listless zombies camp out at slot machines in those sweltering river towns. He conjured this image not in a derogatory sense but rather as a vehicle to appraise himself when transposing his actions onto a more ordinary setting. And, he was certain he was one of the zombies.

Stepping within, the club wasn't as dark as it had seemed from the outside looking in. So many eyes groped at Max that he questioned his prospects of orchestrating a drug deal under such scrutiny. Oh well. He was still feeling the warm surge of his earlier drinks and assumed that many of the sensually swaying bodies around him were in the clutches of ecstasy. But what the hell was *pink*?

Max tunneled through a lively dance floor that seemed to function as an organic whole, a superorganism like an ant colony. A hand squeezed his butt, another pulled on his wrist, and some red lips blew him a kiss. The men in this place smiled more than they had at other bars, and the women looked more earnest. A siren shrieked from vibrating wall speakers and a group of shirtless boys with shaved chests and tanned six-pack abs began dancing in unison to a house-mix version of Cher's "Believe."

Behind one of the bars was, in fact, a handsome man called (according to his nametag) Hadley with yellow highlights in his spikey hair. His tank top revealed bulging biceps—the swollen look one gets walking fresh out of the gym.

"Hey, hun, what can I get for you?" asked Hadley, as Max leaned over the bar.

"Hi, um, so I'm with this girl—named Melpomene." He felt ridiculous saying it out loud. "She's—she's waiting outside, I hope. Anyway, she asked me to find you and see if I could get some 'pink' from you. I—I just have ten bucks on me, so whatever that amount will, um, procure." Max felt like he needed to keep talking until some recognition illuminated the other man, but he had run out of words and hadn't flipped a switch.

"Who?" said Hadley after a considered pause. Max reddened. Benson's cell phone buzzed in his pocket.

"Nevermind, I'm probably in the wrong place. Sorry to bother you."

"Sweetie, she asked you for 'pink'? And she asked you specifically to come to me about this?"

"Yeah, I think so."

"This is a gay bar. She's totally fucking with you."

"Yeah, sure."

"Don't be embarrassed, hun. Girls pull this kind of thing on guys all the time on Bourbon Street. She's probably not going to be outside when you get out there. Girls here feel like guys in this city, tourists I mean, are totally fair game to be fucked with." He placed two shot glasses on the bar and poured from a bottle of Jack Daniels. "Here, don't look so dour. Have a shot—on me."

"Oh, thanks man." They clinked glasses and drank before Max wandered back outside to what he expected to be an empty sidewalk.

"You get it?" Melpomene popped out from a secluded nook between buildings.

"Jesus, you scared me. No, I didn't get it. He had no idea what the hell I was talking about. What is this shit anyway? Why'd you send me in there, what's the point of this?" The phone buzzed again in his pocket. "I gotta call my friend back, so I should probably do that now, unless you have any more important errands for me to run."

"Babe, he knows what it is. It's just that you look like a narc with your white polo and black jeans. He got spooked and didn't want to sell to you." The importunate phone again rattled his thigh. "It's OK, it's OK," she continued. There was a pause as she looked him up and down, seeing him perhaps anew. "Hey— could we go to your hotel room?" She had a way of enunciating each new phrase as if that idea was the point all along.

"I—it's just that my buddy's already asleep in the room."

"Oh, we can be quiet. Come on, take me there. Let's spend the night together." She leaned in for a kiss and pawed around his jeans before landing around the zipper and fondling him purposefully. There was something rushed about her gestures.

"We just can't go there. I'm sorry. I wish we could—trust me." He slid out the phone from the front of his jeans after she pulled away, displaying its firm urgency within his hand. Somehow he felt like only physical evidence could extract him from her clutches at that point.

"Fine. Fine! I suppose—I suppose I could stay at my dad's house tonight." She looked down at the cracked sidewalk. This part of Bourbon Street didn't earn the same attention from the city fathers as the throbbing tourist Mecca closer to Canal. Her eyes had lost their cavernous blackness and electric sheen. Still dark, they now were simply dilated like those of a treed cat. "You got any money I could use for cab fare?"

He gave her the ten-dollar bill and used the cell phone to call a Yellow Cab. They waited nearly thirty minutes for her ride, barely sharing another word. When she finally slipped into the back of the car, he attempted a farewell.

"Nice meeting you. Have fun at your dad's." She tilted her head at him as if she were trying to understand, pausing in the midst of slamming the door.

"Yeah, I hope he doesn't hit me again." And she was off.

Max stood there for a minute, puzzled. This woman was no child, probably older than he was anyway. Was this a final plea to be rescued or one last grift? He checked that his wallet was still safely nestled in its spot and then called Sam.

The crowd at BBC had plateaued around midnight and still had a couple more hours before relenting just before the blood orange dawn. The previous night's band was back and cycling through the same routine: "Get your fuckin' hands up!" Downstairs reverberated with thudding strikes of the bass drum and dozens of bouncing dancers. The air was heavy with a viscous haze of cigarettes and pheromones and smelled of sweet liqueurs. Each step underfoot was sticky, and Max's arms too grew sticky after splashes of pale beer and fragrant red cocktails anointed him during his sortie into the midst of the dancefloor.

There he found Sam, inert, expressionless, a monument to be avoided—or perhaps venerated as a relic by his swarming sybaritic flock.

"What's with the statue routine?"

"I am not a man," said Sam. Upon closer inspection he was actually swaying like a flagellant who had just been struck. "I am worthless as a human being." His hand clung to a plastic cup of beer that he seemed to have given up on, though its frothy liquid periodically spilled over the rim and trickled down his indifferent knuckles.

"Guess I should have come earlier."

"Yeah, that was more than ten minutes. Way more." He was surveilling the room, even the exit. "I fucked up. I talked to her, Electra, for a really long time."

"Well that's—"

"Good, right? You would think! We talked for a really long time, like for real *talked*, and then, well, she was getting off work and she asked me to come with her to another bar—to Razoo's down the street." He jerked his body around to face Max for the first time, splashing the foamy head of his beer like the spume of a cresting wave. A few white gobs spattered onto a young dancing couple. One of the two—a petite, bouncy blonde—kept dancing, utterly unaffected. Her partner, who was taller and sported oaky gelled hair and a soberly clinched jaw, began slapping the substance from their clothes.

"Fuckin' guy. How 'bout you watch what you're

doing when you bring your drunk ass around the dancefloor next time, huh?"

"He's sorry. He's just—he's having a bad night." Max snatched some cocktail napkins from the bar and handed them to the couple. The larger, darker woman ripped them from his hand and began rubbing a handful against her jeans and her partner's red leather miniskirt. Sam was staring off toward the street, not exactly aloof but rather focused on a world out of view.

"I said 'no,'" said Sam, suddenly snapping back into the present.

"What?"

"I don't fucking know! I just did, all right?"

"Listen, man—"

"I don't deserve to be called a man," snapped Sam.

"OK, about Electra," began Max more slowly. He hadn't intended to broach the subject but found immunity within the broad zone of Sam's drunkenness. "Are you sure this girl really exists? I mean 'Electra' is probably just a nametag that they pass around, and all the girls here totally fuck with the guys, I'm sure. *Oh yeah, sure I remember you from last time, sweetie! Buy some drinks for the next two hours and then maybe we'll go spend some time together.* That sort of thing. Listen to me, you're drunk every time you're in this place, and I know you don't have that much experience with alcohol, and you probably see a chick with a nametag that says something similar to that name and you build up in your mind that you've got some relationship brewing with a girl named 'Electra' when in reality that's just a composite of all the crazy ass girls working here, who all kind of resemble the type of girl you haven't yet had in your life." Sam gulped from his beer.

"Jesus, she's fucking real! Are you kidding me? I can tell the difference between a bartender upselling me and real interest. Believe me, she meant what she said."

"Sorry I got held up. I—had a strange time with that girl, and well, I refused to go somewhere with her too."

"Yes, that was more than ten minutes."

"Yeah, I believe we've covered this already."

"Tell me you believe in her and you will not be judged."

"Believe in Electra? Yeah, sure, I don't care."

"So you do believe?"

"Yes, Jesus, now can we get out of here?"

"You, Max Orbach, believe in Electra?"

"I already said, 'Yes,' now can we get the fuck out of here? I'm too broke to buy any more drinks."

"That's three times, you said it three times. That means something."

"OK."

"I made the Jew believe!" He stretched his arms outward in a crucifixion pose, spilling droplets of beer onto the splotchy floor. "It was right there, at the bar here, downstairs, that I talked to her—for like an hour. You are walking on consecrated ground, you Godless Jew. And I mean that in the best of ways because there is no God, of course. I mean there *was* no God—there is now." He began an atavistic swiveling of his hips in the vicinity of a black-haired girl who had been dancing near the two guys and periodically casting sideways smiles. The girl was not opposed to Sam's responsiveness, creeping closer until the two locked together in a wordless swaying trance. Max looked away, sinking, he feared, into the form of cumulative exhaustion and malaise that buries a person who has crammed for exams on consecutive nights, and when he glanced back the two were engaged in a sloppy kiss. As Max began to turn toward the door a hand, claw-like, clasped his shoulder.

"Drink with us." A shot girl, African American with a crimson wig, handed two test tubes each to Max, Sam, and the black-haired girl. She held two herself, and then all four drank the syrupy red liqueur.

"We drink of the blood!" said Sam. He paid and tipped an amount worthy of the *faire la bise* he received from the server. Then, after his dancing partner had wandered off into the night, Sam peered at the remaining foam drops of beer in his cup. He splashed them onto Max's face as the two started toward the exit. "You are now baptized!"

* * *

Back in Atena, Max was now working full-time at Tobacco Bazaar and occasionally mailing his resumé to local newspapers. The *Atena Star*, a subsidiary of the parent news company that owned the Dallas newspaper was a longshot, being staffed almost entirely by Atena State journalism graduates who had landed internships during their senior year, which Max had not. The *Delphin Courier*, however, was a twice weekly paper servicing a farm town thirty minutes north of Atena and offering only a $28,000 salary for a school district beat reporter. Reporter wages seemed to have dropped from even the pessimistic averages discussed by his professors over the past couple years. Springing for pricier resumé paper and a padded manila envelope, he mailed them his application complete with three writing samples, five references, and a cover letter. Jessica, who had grown up in Delphin, knew the rich old man who owned the paper—and his son. She promised to speak to them.

Lately, Max and Jessica were either drinking beers in his bedroom or going to the movies. At the new multiplex out by the old loop they watched the latest M. Night Shyamalan movie, *Signs*. Max loved the reckless thrill of horror movies, especially when paired with the scheduled disorientation of the director's trademark surprises. Jessica felt off balance. She liked the stable niceness of teen dramas and romantic comedies. The trauma was regulated and sanitized enough to remind the audience that the lows would all be reversed in good time. Surprises, whether produced in the punchy form of killers or aliens jumping out from behind the frame or through a twist in the denouement, gave her anxiety. Knowing this, Max at first resolved to seeing *Signs* with Benson, but finally, when making up after a fight, she was feeling magnanimous and suggested they go before it expired from theatres.

Her shallow hand mustered more rangy strength than he would have thought possible, constricting his wrist and digging her little French tip nails into his irritated flesh. It irked him when she took two separate bathroom breaks during the critical scenes and then blankly told him afterward, "It was good or whatever, I think—but I don't know."

"Yeah, it kind of gave me chills, in a good way, when it all came together—the wife's death and battling the aliens and everything."

"Um, yeah, but like I didn't get what she had to do with anything. She was already dead, so what did she have to do with the ending?"

"I think you missed the point—"

"No, yeah, it was good. I just didn't get it."

The earlier fight had been over Slade, the son of the *Delphin Courier* owner, and what exactly had happened at a party years ago.

"We were friends in high school and then he started talking to Tamara and they dated or whatever for a couple months," she had said as if it were an open and shut case for which she was the star witness. "Why do you care?"

"Why? Because he didn't just *date* your God damn big-titted friend." Tamara was a mixed-race Afro-Latina who had politely rejected Benson (and every other of Max's friends). If this Slade character had locked her down for months, then he was trouble. "I've heard you two giggling before about how you've both messed around with him—like it's some damn slutty sisterhood." He was pacing around the cold concrete of his bedroom that shifted from a mild gray tone under the flood of morning light to a coarse charcoal, rough with pools of inky blackness, by evening. Grinding the glowing butt of one cigarette into the stolen glass ashtray that reeked of spent nicotine blended with a dark, reedy earthiness, he immediately lit another.

"Shut up, Max." She twisted open a beer bottle and greedily drank. Max spun around to face her—unused to this direct form of address. "Yes, OK, I fooled around with him exactly one time—at a party—when I was 16, which was two whole years before I met you!" Max jerked open his own beer and gulped, mostly to punctuate his argument, which he felt slipping from him and fermenting into generic meanness.

"The point, Jessica," he said after a glottal sigh, "is that I assumed you were going to speak to the old man about getting me an interview, not some douche whom you—did whatever you did with. Look, I know you meant well, but now I seem like some kind of groveling nullity."

"I don't know what that means. Sometimes I— sometimes I think you intentionally use words I won't know to make me feel dumb. Like that book."

"*The Sun Also Rises*? It's just a book I like. I bought you a copy to be nice, not to make you feel stupid."

"Well I can't read it. I mean I can, but I can't get into it. I don't like the characters, how they talk, how they always want to escape to somewhere else. Why would you think I'd like something like that?"

"Christ, it's just a fucking book! Don't read it for all I care!" And with that she stormed out of his room, slamming the door (which Max considered to be an annoyingly cliché-laced gesture) and stomped through the kitchen, past Benson in the living room, and then sat with the engine running in her car for several minutes before screeching away.

The next day he made her dinner as a goodwill gesture while Benson was out on a date with the new barista at Pluto's. Penelope, the barista, had finally given her number, confusingly, to both Benson and Max when they stumbled in one night with a couple old intramural soccer buddies after the bars closed. Max had done most of the talking, intrigued by her pixie cut that matched her emerald fingernails. She was one of those girls who laughed heartily at any male attempt toward humor and possessed an inner reserve sufficient to observe whatever dark secret a man could entrust to her. Max couldn't picture her with female friends—hosting bridal showers or critiquing dress patterns or high-fiving her swim team buddies—but he could picture sitting beside her on a barstool while his friends hovered around with cups of beer, shifting their weight. Once Benson and Max had returned home that night, his visions of her were hardly germane to the question of who would pocket the receipt with her scribbled phone number, being as only one of the two had a girlfriend. Benson had started law school that fall at Atena State, and Max couldn't help but picture how easily that revelation would roll off his tongue and into her welcoming ears, her corral lips smiling, her green eyes turning upward to lock with his. *Really*, she would breathe. *That's so exciting!* Then a pensive exhale as she reappraised his stock.

The spaghetti sauce was simply Homestyle Ragu, crimson-colored and thickened with chunks of diced tomatoes and dehydrated garlic. The meatballs, by contrast, he made from scratch, employing a recipe his mom had mailed him for a Cajun style. Somehow he felt like importing a Louisiana-inspired cuisine would equate to sharing his recent trip with Jessica and alleviate a bit of the gnawing guilt he felt at leaving her home. The recipe was hardly authentic, essentially adding Zatarain's Creole Seasoning to a standard meatball, but it was one of the most ambitious cooking endeavors Max had thus far attempted, a fact not lost on Jessica who beamed throughout and flipped her stance on seeing *Signs* that night. She even pretended not to notice when he mined his vocabulary a little too deeply in describing the supple features of Benson's date.

* * *

It wasn't until early October that Max heard from the *Delphin Courier*. The kitchen phone rang and didn't display an 800 number for once on the caller ID, so he answered.

"Hey, may I speak to Max Orbach?" said a bored voice on the other end.

"Speaking."

"Yeah, hey man. This is Slade Stevenson at the *Delphin Courier*, and we did get your application for the beat writer position." After a pause: "Jessica talked to me too. Anyway, my dad's gonna wait on interviewing people until December—it's a budget thing, I don't know—but he wants you to call us back then and see if we're ready to bring you in. That cool with you, man?"

Max thanked him and hung up.

* * *

It was a breezy, arid autumn across the North Texas plains, as lawns scorched throughout an Indian summer into brown then shone a pallid yellow beneath the lazy, leaden sky. On a Friday in early November, Max leaned against the smudged glass case at Tobacco Bazaar listening to a local AM sports radio show with Andrew. They had tuned in to catch a segment with Atena State's head football coach—who rarely logged any airtime in the Dallas/Fort Worth media market, perennially buried beneath Cowboys analysis and seldom able to claw into even the college football conversations, dominated as they were by the three-headed Cerberus of Oklahoma, Texas, and Texas A&M. Today, though, five minutes was magnanimously preserved for Coach Fry Mitchell who had positioned his team to reach bowl eligibility on Saturday with a win against the University of Louisiana. Atena State hadn't been to a bowl game in a generation, and the attrition from decades of losing had fractured the once-proud fanbase into tiny, isolated pockets and odd pairings, such as the two Tobacco Bazaar employees. The show hosts—who spoke to Mitchell the way a hip young teacher talks to a bullied, underdeveloped freshman before mocking his shrill voice in the faculty lounge—ended the segment with an awkward hypothetical: "So, Coach, how do ya 'spose your boys'd match up with the Longhorns if ya clashed with them in yer bowl game there?" His co-host joined him in a tired chuckle.

Mitchell, nearing retirement, had been one of the first African American players to integrate Division 1 college football in Texas in the late 1950s—signing with an unheralded Atena State team after the Longhorns and Aggies had passed and filled their backfields with white running backs. "Well, boys, we've got a couple guys who can run the ball with hurricane force, and I think we could do some damage to their defensive line—if we are so fortunate as to earn the opportunity."

Following the segment was an AP news brief. The United Nations had unanimously approved Resolution 1441, which compelled Saddam Hussein's Iraq to disarm or face invasion.

"No one's going to do shit," said Andrew. "Bush'll fire some Patriot missiles like his dad to show everyone he's still got a dick, but he's too afraid of losing the support of Senate Democrats."

"He's got all the power, though. Daschle and most of the others handed the car keys over to old Gin and Tonic. They don't want the responsibility of crafting a nuanced bill, so they just passed the War Resolution Act and put their faith in a dude who can barely identify Iraq on a map." Walt came into the store front from the humidor with his hard pack of Marlboro Reds jutting out of the pocket of his crisscrossed Ceylon flannel shirt. He'd been protractedly smoking down a dark, Cameroon-leaf Cohiba Churchill since the morning and reeked of a moist earthiness like fern.

"Walter, tell the kid here that we needed to pass the War Resolution Act," said Andrew, who folded his arms and leaned his sweaty back against the sallow wall. His gut dropped down past his jagged belt buckle, which contained his neatly tucked polo.

"Oh, I don't know about invading Iraq. If we find out that they *did* have something to do with 9-11 then sure, let's blast the bastards no matter how many pussy-ass college students walk out of class to protest—or whatever they're doing these days—like *that's* supposed to accomplish anything. But, on the other hand, if Tom Daschle doesn't see the evidence, then I happen to think he ought to have some spine and stand up to Dubya." Max mumbled a note of approval but was searching the mall hallway where a familiar form caught his attention.

"Walter, come on, Senator Daschle's an Air Force

man like you." Andrew snatched a napkin left from his lunch, a Dave's Triple meal from Wendy's, and dabbed at a swath of sweat across his forehead. His face always seemed to be damp and stubbly with dark whiskers that somehow sprouted by the end of his shift.

"Heh," chuckled Walter with some effort. "I do tell people that, don't I?" Walter was a dying breed, a Blue Dog Democrat in Texas. He'd fallen in love with LBJ in the Sixties and been seeking a man of that mold ever since. Bush wasn't far off in his vernacular, but his inner constitution was all wrong. Walter couldn't get past his Evangelical rhetoric. It was the same face he put on in front of Tobacco Bazaar customers, but Bush really seemed to believe his schtick, which Walter couldn't understand. At the same time, Bush's hokey southern twang and performances clearing brush from his Crawford ranch seemed embarrassingly curated. Religion, to Walt, was something worth lying about, a front for women or small children: dabbling in lapidary arts to smooth over humanity's cruel edges for the beautiful innocents.

"At least Ted Kennedy and some of the New England Dems still have some spine," added Max with his eyes fixed on the store entrance, hoping to get another glimpse at the specter who had stoked his memory—a female form. One of Jessica's friends? Hopefully not. A girl from one of his classes? Maybe someone from the Journalism Department?

"Oh, fuck those piss ants," bellowed Andrew. "Remind me never to set foot in that Commie part of the country. They oughta kick Lincoln Chaffee out of the GOP for voting with the Democrats; that traitorous mother fucker looks like a Seventies anti-war hippie, like some Kent State agitator."

"Andy, don't get too heated now. It's almost the Friday rush, and I don't need you sweatin' like a whore in church, especially if some of the wives come in with them." Walter popped a cigarette into his mouth and was already inching back toward the humidor as he was speaking. He preferred to evade Andrew's conversational entreaties unless a customer served as witness.

"You guys are way too nice. We can't afford to be nice in the twenty-first century. Saddam, Iraq, Iran, Afghanistan—all a part of Al-Qaeda, all a network. That Atena mosque, you know the mother fuckers I'm talking about, outside of the loop, they're a sleeper cell. They *all* are!"

"Yeah, hang on a second, Andrew." Max darted for the hallway.

"Excuse me, hey, Penelope!" Max had finally placed the silhouette who had been roving up and down the main mall thoroughfare, recognizing her bony torso from behind despite her hair having devolved from green to jet black. She was with a friend.

"Huh," she turned sharply around. "Oh, you're Benson's roommate, right?" The friend also inspected the intruder with what was nearly amusement. She was fuller of figure than Penelope, older maybe, and sported a Medusa tattoo that was visible through the sheer, gauzy back of her black blouse.

"Yeah, that's right. Actually we met at Pluto's."

"Oh, you were with him. How is Benson anyway? It's been awhile." Although he had never said it, Max assumed Benson had slept with her after a prolonged Saturday night second date.

"He's been—he's always studying these days. Law school, guess it's kicking his ass a little bit." The friend smirked.

"Oh sorry, this is Clytie; and, Clytie, this is—"

"Max."

"Max! Fuckin' Max," said Clytie, who had been studying him, first with anthropological interest and then something else. She carried her sturdy frame (she was at least half a foot taller than her friend and with broader shoulders) whimsically—like all of the silly men and women with classically sexy bodies were being cosmically pranked. Her face was round and pale, contrasting with the elongated black lines that dripped past the corners of her eyes and her dark hair that plunged endlessly down her back. She carried a sensual confidence that churned not with some effective feminine shapeliness but from behind her sideways smile. The matte black contour that encircled and accented her grey eyes amplified her facial expressions in a way that precluded speech.

"It's lovely to meet you," said Max, extending a hand. He never spoke to women with any great panache and wondered where a word like "lovely" came from.

"Dude," began Penelope, "We're going to check out Hot Topic for a sec. I know, I know, such a cliché for emo girls to shop at Hot Topic, but fuck it. Anyway, I don't know if Benson's totally over me or whatever, but if you guys are up for it, Clytie and I are going to hit up this karaoke joint out on Lake Saronic, so yeah— come hang with us. If you want. Whatever, it's cool either way." She cocked her head toward her friend who sprang a nod. "Oh!" She clapped her hands and held them in front of her chest. "I don't have a cell phone, but you should give your number to Clytie, Max." Her tongue sort of lingered on the final "s" sound of his name.

"Yes." Clytie spoke for the first time. I'll call you, Max." She smiled at Penelope. "Come sing with us!"

* * *

The phone rang more than three times before Jessica picked up, a rarity since about their first month of dating. This was a good sign, Max interpreted, and when other jangly giggles were audible in the background, this was even better.

"Max? Hey, what are you doing? Tamara, oh my God, *no* you *have* to wear that, it's so silly—sorry, Max, hang on a sec, will ya?" Distant from the receiver but projected like an off-Broadway actor was Tamara's voice: "No, you skank! I look like a frumpy minivan carpool mom—or, in other words, my mother. What are *you* wearing? What *is* that, a tube top, huh Jessticle?" More giggling. The name was an inside joke between the two of them to which Max had never been privy—not that he wanted to know, given the reddening of her face whenever Tamara said it.

"Oh my God, Tamara's being so funny! We're 'spose to go to this stupid party tonight, so we're up in her bedroom trying on clothes and drinking Malibu and Coke." Then, after a pause that may have only felt significant, "You can come—it's just that it's—in Delphin, you know? Some guys we know from high school have a house—mainly Tamara's friends." In the background: "They're your friends too!"

"Yeah, you know what, Jess? That's not really my

scene. You two have fun, and I'll probably just hang here with Benson or something." In effect, it was the dream scenario. And, he almost embraced his good fortune, if not for something dark that churned within his breast and floated up his larynx and fluttered his tongue to life: "Is Slade going to be there?"

"Well, yes, he's the one who invited us—I mean he told Tamara about the party, and she wanted me to come along, you know?"

"Right."

"It's nothing weird, if you're thinking—well I don't know what. He's giving us a ride so we don't have to drive drunk. Isn't that a nice thing to do?"

"He's an Eagle Scout. Have fun with your boyfriend." He hung up.

She didn't call back.

When the house phone finally rang a few hours later and showed an unfamiliar number, Max snagged it before Benson could intercept him. Clytie, shouting over the uneven ruckus of a karaoke lounge, was imploring the guys to hurry down there, as they had both already signed up to sing and apparently needed the bulwark of a male cheering section. She repeated herself several times, which Max attributed to the ambient cacophony—but could have been something else.

For Max, the problem was this: He and Benson had argued—in that evasive, halting, pointless way that young men do—to a stalemate regarding their evening. Benson's position was that he couldn't in good conscience see Penelope again without misleading her as to his intent, which was nil (he had turned his attentions to a Legal Ethics classmate with creamy pale

skin, a blond ponytail, and dogged research acumen).
Max felt that a friendly karaoke bar meetup on the lake
would be in no way injurious to any interested party.
Fearing, however, an awkward rescinding of the girls'
invitation, he feigned ignorance as to the other's
disinterest, and informed Clytie they were on their way.

As it turns out, Max's time at Lake Saronic was
brief. The girls were yelling at a chiseled thirty-
something man wearing an olive US Army t-shirt,
snakeskin cowboy boots, and a shaved head.

"They killed MY brothers, those towel-head
mother fuckers, and I am ready to go kick some camel-
jockey's teeth in the second Bush sends my ass over to
that shithole country!"

"Move it along, folks. All three of you. Gotta go!"
A bouncer with outstretched arms was attempting to
corral the three toward the door, while also shielding
the man from the girls.

"You couldn't even fucking point out Iraq on a
map, you ignorant swine!" Penelope shouted.

"Fucking fascist—er racist!" Clytie contributed.
She barely resembled the composed, serene girl from
the mall a few hours earlier.

"I tell you what—" He was glaring, red-faced and
wolfish, at Penelope. "I may not pass some gay
geography quiz, but when I sneak up on one of those
sand-eating mother fuckers and shove the barrel of my
Colt M4 up his ass, he'll sure as fuck know where *I*
am!"

"Move, MOVE." The bouncer was now shoving
him out the door. A couple more security goons swam
through the sea of bodies around the bar and began
pushing and prodding the girls toward a second exit—

with Max sheepishly following behind. The bar extended on stilts a good ways over the lake, and he felt like he could feel the errant churn of moonlit waters below his feet, tossing recklessly back and forth.

"Don't touch my ass, dude," said Penelope to a neckless, hulking gorilla of a man. He was tanned to a loud orange, like he'd been dipped in amber, and revealed bulging veins around his enormous biceps through an ill-fitted staff t-shirt.

"I'll grab whatever I wanna grab, sweetheart, if you girls can't behave."

"I should probably drive you two home, right?" said Max once they found themselves in the parking lot.

Being amped up with adrenaline, they fumed, and laughed, and plotted during the ride home—barely recognizing Benson's absence. The whooping within the car continued after they parked just past the town square and stumbled up the stairs to Penelope's apartment, which was one of four units residing above a downtown bookstore. A couple male neighbors, college-aged, heard the commotion and emerged from their front door across the hall to greet this group of two tottering girls and one sober fool who trailed behind. One of the guys looked a bit older up close, maybe late twenties or early thirties and balding. His stomach was plump beneath a beige Atena State hoodie, and he smelled fresh—like he'd just showered with gardenia-scented soap. The other was taller, fitter, but a bit smarmy and with rank breath that had almost a bitter yeastiness to it.

"Sup, Penny?" said the second man, issuing a blast of stale breath. Damn, thought Max, he must have just polished off about a hundred cheap beers to have built up that foulness. "You girls been out tonight? You wanna pop in for some drinks?" Then to Max: "Hey, bro. Name's Cal." He extended a hand without veering focus from Penelope. "Come over, Penny, we got Shiner, Jack Daniels, you name it." He was swaying a bit and appeared to be squeezing out a smile that faltered halfway across his face and hung instead as an idiotic sneer. "You're Clytie, right? I seen you around few times before." He scanned her up and down.

"Yes, Cal, we've met a couple times," she replied, flashing a look at Max that he didn't understand.

"Dude, we had a shit night—probably gonna just hang out at home a bit and then pass out," said Penelope.

"Yeah, I should let you guys get to sleep," said Max. He began to turn back down the stairs but was arrested by Clytie's hand gripping his wrist.

"You stay." It was almost a whisper and was accompanied by an urgency in her eyes that again bewildered him.

"Cal, man, we should let these folks get to bed. Come on inside," said the chubby roommate.

"Dude, you go to bed." He edged a little bit closer to Penelope and her door. "Please, Penny. Maybe I could jump in there to your place for a drink with you. Just one and then I'll piss off. Come on, we never hangout anymore!"

"OK, whatever, come in guys. We can't stand out here yapping away any longer or we'll wake up all our other boring neighbors. But don't blame me if I sneak off to bed and pass out after one drink."

Once inside, Cal found Penelope's stereo and cranked on some blistering hardcore punk from a CD that he snatched out of its sleeve, after thumbing violently through an unzipped case. He disappeared for a few minutes and then returned with a punch that he had mixed together with "just a splash of Everclear." Reluctantly, at first, Penelope and Clytie gulped a few cups of the red concoction. Max drank beers from the refrigerator and sank down into the brown cushions next to Clytie, whose drooping eyelids betrayed a wooziness that Max had not recognized just an hour earlier. Cal was propping up Penelope, almost like a marionette, to keep her alert and dancing with him up until she broke loose and stumbled across the room, falling twice, before finally switching off the stereo.

"Welp, that's our cue to leave, Cal," said the roommate.

"You go to bed. I'm cool, man. Just going to hang here for a bit and say good night to Penny." Clytie drooped her head with finality against Max's shoulder and respired noisily as if dreams had seized swiftly into her. One minute she had been coherently, even eloquently, dissecting the TV networks' coverage of recent major events (from the usurpation of the 2000 Presidential Election to 9/11)—convinced that the major media outlets' narrative framing was flimsy, irresponsible, and reflective only of the audience's biases—and then she described the room as spinning and could barely enunciate her words. The last thing she said to him before passing out was either "drunk" or "weak." He couldn't tell. Penelope sloshed down the hallway to her bedroom, pawing for balance against the dark walls, making some frowning guttural exclamation before slamming her door shut. They could hear her spill onto the bed like groceries from an over-taxed bag that has ripped open.

"Cal, listen," said his friend in a hushed tone. Max had closed his eyes in solidarity with Clytie but wasn't yet asleep. "These girls are really drunk. Know what I mean?" He hesitated and perhaps sighed before crossing the exterior hallway back to the other apartment, leaving Cal pacing in Penelope's living room. Struggling to process the devolved dynamic of the party, Max simply kept closed his eyes and brushed aside any marauding thoughts as the other man's footsteps pattered away toward the lone bedroom. Recognizing his newfound privacy with Clytie, who was pressed up against him with an unconscious hand dangling near his crotch. Delicately, he reached up his right hand and switched off the towering lamppost that glowed, bulbous, in the corner. Yellow moonlight gushed through a narrow window and painted the pair anew, erasing the spurts of wan electric light that had blandly blanketed the room. In this new light, Clytie— serenely unaware—glowed a brilliant chartreuse, while the same light only reached parts of Max, leaving his left half cloaked in darkness. He looked her over and gently whisked long bangs from her eyes with his right hand. A rustling sound from down the hallway didn't quite seem in tune with Penelope's presumed unconsciousness, and Max wondered weakly why this Cal was bothering her for so long with his "goodbye." But, a vague instinct jolted through him as he noticed the exposed skin of Clytie's thigh smoothly brushed up against the palm of his left hand. His fingers, mindless, crept upward a bit toward the hem of her shorts that flopped open enough to have accommodated a surreptitious hand. A distant noise, neither human nor animal, a grousing alto of sorts, jostled his ears into attention, and he twisted his head toward the window, basking now fully in the moon's glow. There was something about the sound that pricked him. Roused now from his previous impulse and seized by a more ancient instinct, he pulled his hand from her thigh and was ashamed. Then it hit him. Penelope.

He rushed down the hallway and flung open the door to see Cal fumbling with the buttons of her shorts and trying to peel off the clingy denim from her flesh. She was shirtless already with her arms flailed outward, etherized and limp. Her eyelids were half lifted and her open mouth groaned in wordless distress. Cal turned at him, faceless, a black silhouette perched upon her bed.

"I'm just helping her undress," he said. "We're all good in here, man."

"Bullshit," said Max before fully comprehending the path he was taking. "Come on, she's passed out, probably should leave her alone, huh?"

"Mind your business, man. Go titty fuck that fat one out there or something. I got dibs on Penny—you got your own chick out there."

"No way. You gotta go." Cal stood, looming, several inches taller than Max.

"The fuck you gonna do about it, little man?" he bellowed. Max found it strange that Cal wasn't particularly concerned about waking the girls.

"Come on, just go home and let her sleep. This doesn't have to turn into a whole thing." He hoped his affected neutral tone could diffuse the other's inflating anger, but instead Cal approached him. Max braced himself, as he did not believe he was likely to win a fight with the larger man. On the other hand, he figured he could hold his own long enough for the girls to wake up amid the fray.

"Fuckin' pussy," said Cal while shoving him with both hands in the sternum so that he flew away from the door's opening and clunked into the wall. Max balled his fingers into fists and prepared for the next onslaught, but instead Cal simply sulked down the hall and out the front door.

At home the next morning, Benson was playing back the answering machine for Max. "Listen to this shit. It kept waking me up, yelling, just a bunch of yelling—first at 3:33 in the morning, then like four more every couple minutes." They hit "Play" and sure enough there were a slew of ranting, screaming, cackling messages of Jessica and Tamara in concert with occasional background voices in lower tones.

"Jesus, sorry about her drunk ass. I'll talk to her later—when they've had time to sleep it off—wherever they are." He thought for a second. "Listen, you wanna go to the Atena State game today? I'm supposed to meet Andrew there, the guy from work, but—you know how he is. I need a third party there."

"Can't do it, I have to study today. You're on your own with Andrew."

"So it looks like we'll be playing in a bowl game in New Orleans if we win today. If I'm not starting a new job with that newspaper, I might try to go. You wanna go back there?"

"Nah, man, I had my fill of that trash city. Plus, I need to save money—apparently you're flush with cash."

"Ha, yeah. Well, Sam's been calling and asking about it for a couple weeks now. Guess we could probably make it a pretty cheap trip if we're careful—if I have nothing else going on, of course."

"You two are on your own."

* * *

Sitting behind the north endzone at Atena Stadium, Andrew crunched on ballpark nachos and dropped pickled jalapenos onto the empty bleacher in front of him. The two sat silently throughout much of the first quarter, focused instead on a game that was closely contested and defined by turnovers. The quarter ended with a misleading 7-7 score, which was comprised of two defensive scores—one a fumble return for a touchdown by a Louisiana linebacker who had just thumped unconscious the quarterback. An Atena State defensive back later tied the game by intercepting and returning an errant Louisiana pass, a miscommunication between the quarterback and receiver on a broken play.

"So, I broke up with Jess," said Max during the timeout between quarters.

"No shit?" Andrew gulped his Diet Coke and wiped greasy fingers across his khaki shorts. His legs were nearly hairless, like a swimmer's, but it was hard to imagine his pale arms thrashing about in any Olympic-sized pool.

"Yep. She got really drunk last night and apparently ended up sleeping over with this Slade douchebag."

"So she fucked him? This douche?"

"She says she just slept in his bed—that her friend Tamara hooked up with this other guy and so the only place to sleep at Slade's apartment was conveniently in his bed."

"Please tell me you don't believe that shit, son?"

"I don't know, maybe. It doesn't matter. She drinks so much with this crowd from high school and then ends up in compromising situations. The point is that I don't want to always *have* to guess about whether I believe her or not."

"These little bitches, man. Most of them are snakes, especially the Mexican chicks. They try to see what they can get out of you—size you up—and then bleed you dry, leave you with nothing. On to the next victim—someone richer, always someone richer. It never goes the other direction."

"Yeah, you're probably right." He looked up at the slate gray sky that held muted pools of sunlight behind a nictitating membrane of clouds. The game resumed. A blond cheerleader with green and white ribbons in her bobbed hair ran up and down the sideline in front of the student section waving a pompom. "Hey, Andrew, so I have a question for you." Trombones with their slides extended blared low bestial moans from golden bells. "I'm thinking about taking a trip to New Orleans in December, and I need to make some extra cash between now and then. Do you think I could take some of your shifts? I wouldn't ask except that Walter's cut back my hours so much that I can barely make rent as it is." Before Andrew could answer, a wave of cheers crackled through the stands and most of the section popped onto their feet to watch Baghel Enkidu, the Atena State running back, break loose for a 66-yard touchdown run. The marching band stood to play the fight song in perfect rectilinear columns like a Roman legion.

"That's what I'm talkin' about. Hell yeah!" Andrew turned around and high-fived a stranger in the row behind, a teenager who smirked to his girlfriend and folded his arms as soon as the interloper turned back. "Now Max, I know you don't expect me to give up my paycheck so that you can take a trip. Oh, and Walter's cut back your hours because you're always so late. I gotta take my shifts seriously because I got real responsibilities."

"No, I mean I get it."

"Don't worry, I've got money. Don't worry about me. But—and let this be a lesson to you—I have to pay huge wads of child support to my baby mama so that she can continue to sit on her ass and generally be useless."

"Yeah, no I understand. It's just—I was hoping to go to the bowl game in New Orleans—if we make it. And, you know what?—I actually might not be able to if I start this new job at a newspaper next month. I'm supposed to hear back soon."

"OK, OK, fuck it. If we win this game and are headed to a bowl game in New Orleans, I'll give up some shifts for you. Now don't say I never did anything for ya, son. Ha!"

With bowl eligibility in the balance during the fourth quarter, Atena State began the final drive trailing by four and physically depleted. Their line had been manhandled all afternoon, and their receivers were beginning to collapse all over the field into crumpled balls of cramps after sprinting fruitlessly time and again up and down the field as the defensive front seven continuously disrupted their routes.

"Max Orbach?" A voice a few rows off echoed

across the gray bleachers. Andrew's dampened forearm nudged him toward the game. The quarterback, Gil Gagne, heaved a wobbly pass to the sideline thirty yards downfield. It was the longest completion of the day and was nearly intercepted—hanging perilously long in the air, tossed by the thick November wind as if by a mad juggler.

"Max! It *is* you," said the voice, a young woman's musically importunate tone.

"What are you looking around for, you God-damned kike!" The game's this way." He was nearly angry. In reality, the game was reaching its climax, as Atena State had advanced to the red zone with seconds left and no timeouts.

"Remember me?" said a freckled girl who was climbing over bleachers toward him. "We were in Amnesty International together." The center snapped the ball to Gagne, who was in a pistol formation but dropped back almost to the twenty-yard line, trapped as he was in a collapsing pocket. A sack would end it. "Or, I mean you came once to a letter-writing campaign. Hmm, can't remember which one that was."

"Amnesty?" Max tripped upon a dull recognition, a date who'd once brought him to a meeting in the Student Union, a campaign he hadn't quite understood but jumped into nonetheless.

"Yeah, you remember!" She beamed before him. She was the president of the club, or some sort of officer. But what was her name? A Louisiana defensive tackle, Heath Bull, was upon Gagne and about to pounce when the wildly galloping Baghel Enkidu threw his body in front of Bull's legs, violently taking him down.

110

"Oh shit! He got the pass off," yelled Andrew, hopping to his feet and squeezing Max's shoulder.

"Hattie!" Max remembered her name.

"Touchdown, motherfuckers!" Andrew was bouncing his hulking torso up and down amid a cheering crowd. Even Hattie turned toward the field for a moment.

"So you *do* remember me," she said, fixing her attention again on Max. The final whistle sounded, and the entire Atena State bench was spilling onto the field. Enkidu and Bull lay motionless on the turf, crumpled together in a heap until Gagne helped his running back to his feet. The two limped together in a single-armed embrace with their other fists in the air, ambling victoriously toward their celebrating compatriots in the middle of the field, while Bull yet writhed about, clutching his knee.

"Of course! I always meant to join your club, but I had an evening class during your meetings." He wondered, who is she here with? She had a boyfriend at the time, but there was something so earnest and honest about those cerulean eyes that he was convinced she was seeing him anew.

Andrew was slapping his back and laughing as the two of them marched through the concourse amid other revelers leaving the stadium.

"Well, shit. Aren't you a lucky bastard? You get to go to our bowl game in New Orleans *and* you managed to Jew me out of some work shifts. Must be nice!" He was smiling with a toothy, wolfish mouth.

"Come on, Andrew. Don't say that to me."

"No, you're right, you're right. Sorry about that. I'm just pumped, that's all."

"Yeah, I know what you mean. I'm excited too." It was true enough, as he was eager to plan his return to New Orleans with Sam, but in the foreground of his mind, he was disappointed with himself: in the maelstrom of celebration he had somehow, despite eventually nurturing a healthy conversation, neglected to get Hattie's phone number.

* * *

One morning in early December, the phone rang, jostling Max from a vexing nightmare. He was again dreaming of Hernando de Soto, who this time was pacing up and down the banks of the Mississippi shouting in unintelligible bursts of Spanish gibberish. His men, Max apparently being one of them, understood that the conquistador was mad with fever, but they just let him rant endlessly, whether out of grave respect or abusive neglect. De Soto then scampered up the tipi-like, triangular trunk of a bald cypress tree whose roots reached down into the river and shouted at his men, this time apparently in English: "Don't let them know!" He plucked from a branch a noose that had been stashed within a packet of green needle leaves. "Don't let them know I'm not a god!" And with that, he fastened the noose around his neck and jumped. Max, adjusting suddenly to his reality, took a deep breath to clear his head, having noticed the name on the caller ID.

"Hello," said Max, hoping to hide any traces of his dusty mind.

"Well hello, may I speak to a Mr. Max Orbach?"

"Yes, speaking, hi—I mean, this is Max—hello."

"Great! Max, my name is Cooter Stevenson, and I am calling from the *Delphin Courier* about the school district beat reporter position for which you applied this fall. As you probably know, I'm the owner and editor-in-chief and, well, I spoke to Slade about your impressive application that he brought to my attention. Max, your writing sample really stood out to me. You have an ability to weave a story out of nothing— excellent diction, strong narrative elements overall— maybe a bit too much of a stylized voice for news reporting, but we can work on that. Looks like you were a great student as well, nice GPA."

"Thank you."

"And, I understand that a couple of Slade's friends have vouched for you as well. That goes a long way, you know!"

"Yes."

"So, Max, I just want to further discuss the position with you and ask a few questions and see if we can move forward. This isn't an interview. It's just an opportunity for us to chat and talk about the position and then see where we are. Sound good?"

"Yes, of course."

"Great. Max, first I want to make sure I'm pronouncing your last name correctly. Is it 'Bach' like the composer? But with an 'Or' in front of it?"

"That's right. Thank you for asking."

"Perfect! Such an interesting name. You don't hear many German names around this part of the state. Now, in the Hill country it's quite common, as I'm sure you know, but not around North Texas. Do you know any of the families that go to Temple Emanu-El? A couple of our advertisers happen to be members there."

"No, I'm sorry, I'm afraid I've never been there. Actually, only my father's Jewish. My mother was raised Catholic but now she is an—" He interrupted himself. "She isn't particularly religious. And since my father isn't really a practicing Jew, I only went to synagogue a few times with my grandparents when I was growing up."

"Oh, great, great. So, where did you grow up, Max? Where does the Orbach clan hail from?"

"Well, my parents live nearby in Martha. That's where I went to high school and mostly grew up."

"Oh, sure. They have good schools down in Martha, strong football program. Great place to grow up. But, I mean originally. Your family isn't originally from Texas, I presume."

"No, I see. No, I suppose none of us is a native Texan. My grandparents on my father's side both immigrated as teenagers to New York City from Bohemia in the 1920s and then eventually got married and settled in Cincinnati where my father was born during World War Two. He was still living in Cincinnati, working as a chemist for Proctor and Gamble, when he met my mom, who was an undergrad at Xavier University at the time. To be honest, I don't know much about my maternal grandparents—I mean I never met them. Anyway, like my father, I was born in Cincinnati, but we moved to Martha when I was young."

"Well fantastic, Max. Such a rich backstory you've got. Don't ever forget where you came from!" He coughed viciously. "Excuse me." More coughs, then sputtering laughter. "Now, Max, I suppose I should fill you in on some developments pertaining to this position." There was something stilted about his voice. There was only a trace of a southern accent, but his voice sported the elongated vowel sounds of rich West Texas oilmen. He was either digging up an unnatural folksy twang—or he was suppressing a real one. "What they may or may not have taught you in the journalism department at Atena State is the cold hard fact that the business isn't what it used to be. We just don't have access to the same revenue streams that we used to, and while I had high hopes for this position to be a full-time, salaried job, I simply don't think that's going to be tenable at this time. I tell you what, let's circle back to this conversation after the start of the new year, and we'll see where things stand then. Most likely, we'll be discussing ways for you to contribute to our paper from time to time as a freelance writer. Sound good?"

"Um, sure, well thank you for your time."

"Take care, Max."

"Goodbye." He hung up.

If the world wasn't yet going to admit him into adulthood, then he wouldn't beg. He thought this as he picked the phone back up and called Sam.

* * *

A couple weeks later, Sam and Max sat in the small lobby of U-Lube, located on University Drive near the interstate, waiting for workers to finish up with Max's old Camry. A glossy magazine cover on the table in front of them showed a shirtless Travis Barker perched behind his drum set. His torso was sinewy and sweaty, and his long arms were drenched in sleeves of ink.

"Of all the times to get your oil changed, you had to pick right now. As we were about to leave town. This couldn't wait until we after the trip?" Sam had his arms crossed within a red windbreaker and he was almost doubled over onto his black sweatpants. His biceps were more inflated each time Max saw him, their outline being visible even through two layers of fabric.

"We shouldn't even be taking my car. We'll be lucky if we make it to New Orleans without the old piece of junk overheating or something. If I could afford it, we would be doing far more than just getting the oil changed before setting sail on I-20. This was the bare minimum." He was still examining the magazine cover while speaking. Did women prefer the skinny punk look now? Max patted a hand against his own russet hair to ensure that the pomade he had spread through it earlier that morning was still lifting it up a bit from his scalp. He had also been jogging for the past several weeks in preparation for the trip and its demands upon his body. Having arbitrarily set a goal of running a 50-minute 10K on the treadmill at the Atena State Rec Center, he had progressed easily toward it during the first couple weeks but then had plateaued. Whenever he reached the second half of the 10K, the final 3.1 miles, he would have to slow his pace to a trajectory that wouldn't allow him to finish anywhere close to his 50-minute goal. In fact, usually he just gave up before the final mile.

"Yes. But, why did you wait until the last minute?" He looked at his watch. "Christ, we were supposed to leave in the morning. Now we're way behind schedule."

"I had to wait until I got my paycheck, which was

this morning." Funny, thought Max, throughout his adult life the answer to any question of *why* always involved a paycheck. "Anyway, relax, it's still morning."

"No, No. I meant *early* in the morning—like the crack of fucking dawn. We were supposed to get there by the afternoon, now it's going to be evening." An attractive woman in her 30s or 40s with short black hair approached the service desk. Max was unsure if she was Asian or a Latina. Sam was also studying her.

"What difference does it make? We'll still get there in plenty of time to go out tonight."

"Yes, but that's not—" His concentration was breaking. "It's—we have to get there before the afternoon crew disperses. She might be working during the day."

"It's making kind of a humming noise and vibrating when I turn the wheel," said the black-haired woman to the U-Lube associate behind the register.

"Hmm, yeah that could actually be the brakes," replied the tall, smiling employee, whose nametag said, "Ana."

"Look, I'm at least dressed and ready to go out the second we get there," said Max. "You're in sweatpants."

"That's exactly what I was thinking!" said the black-haired customer. "I've stuck to all of the scheduled maintenance, but I'll confess that I've put off replacing the front brake pads." The two women laughed confidentially. Max did not understand the joke.

"My shirt and pants are hanging in a dry-cleaning bag in the backseat of your piece of shit vehicle. That way they won't get wrinkled while sitting in a car for seven hours. I can change and be ready in no time at all when we finally arrive. You, on the other hand, are going to take forever fixing your hair."

"I said I'm ready to go out," began Max. He noticed the woman with black hair smirking toward them. Lowering his voice to little more than a whisper, he added, "I just have to touch it up with the pomade when we get there—five minutes tops."

"You're still going to the bowl game tomorrow?"

"Well, yeah, that's the whole point of the trip."

"Not for me it isn't," snapped Sam. "I don't understand the point of actually going to the Superdome and wasting an entire afternoon—especially since we're pissing away today. You could just watch it at the bar. I don't see the attraction of witnessing it live."

"There's a certain solidarity in being there in the stadium. I guess I can kind of relate to the Atena State football team."

"You can?"

"Yep. They're underdogs, just like us."

"Us? We're underdogs? Who are we up against?

"Ourselves."

* * *

The bartender at BBC poured without looking, never breaking eye contact with the woman, a friend, seated before her at the bar. Guys, an older crowd this time of day, barked orders at her, some offering "friendly" advice before returning to their half-dazed families (in town from Arkansas or somewhere else lacking the boiling heat that couldn't quite manage to expunge the previous night's liquor and po'boys). Serving politely enough, she only contorted her body to snatch bottled beers and sanitized pint glasses, her gaze unaffected.

"She hangs out in the Marigny," Callie said. "Does roller derby, plays drums in a punk band."

"Rowena's in a band?" the friend asked.

"Totally—they're pretty kick ass. No, Amber, seriously. They packed like a hundred people into the Whirling Dervish for a show on Thursday. A freakin' *Thursday*!"

"But she doesn't act punk. Like her hair is that long poofed-up blond mess. I mean she's pretty and all but not in a punk chick sort of way."

"I know, I know." She didn't even wait for an order this time—just anticipated and clanked down two more Abitas for a sweaty middle-aged man in tan cargo shorts, black Adidas flipflops, and white tube socks. "Rowena looks like Phoebe from *Friends*."

"That's it! That's fucking it," said Amber with the sort of joy that erupts from a friend's implicit understanding.

For his part, Max was bewildered. The characters who populated Bourbon Street—those who found a way to actually *live* in or around the French Quarter, the women especially, didn't seem like they could exist in the same universe as primetime network television. To him, New Orleans was an island nation, an overseas territory at best. The staff at places like this were natives whose reckless smiles and nocturnal habits should be studied by an ethnographer.

Sam stomped down the stairs, brushed past Max with a half nod, then leaned stiffly against the bar. He stood within earshot of the two girls' conversation but far enough not to trigger service from the bartender. After staring at the bulky TV suspended in the corner (they hadn't yet updated to flat screens) and miming interest in the scrolling basketball scores on ESPN, he found his opening.

"Oh, hey, so you both work on Bourbon?" Callie turned toward him. Amber sipped her iced tea.

"She waits tables at Red Fish Grill," said Callie. Amber lit a cigarette and turned away like a diffident child, blowing smoke toward the street. "What do you wanna drink?"

"Bud Light, I guess. And, um, I'll just close out with that." He handed her a debit card.

"You shitting me, dude? You gonna order one beer and make me run a card for that?" The bartender, Callie, didn't appear to be joking. Amber laughed, suddenly interested.

"Sorry, no cash on me," he lied. Max wondered what else was going on.

"Man, you don't got a few bucks on you? You need to drag yo'self to an ATM to survive around here," said Amber. "Don't walk around Bourbon Street broke." She had braided strands that bounced against her face when she spoke, and her brunette hair alternated between caramel and golden, depending on when she dipped into streams of light from the afternoon sun that now flooded through the bar's front entry.

"We're slow, so no biggie. But listen, dude, if you pulled that shit during Mardi Gras most of the girls here would tell you to get the fuck out." Callie slid him the open bottle, which was already beaded with moisture.

A professional couple who had been sitting at a lonely table outside of the bartender's purview stood up with a start and scraped their stools across the floor up to the bar, sufficiently rousing Callie from her brittle interest in Sam's uneven conversational strategy. They were late middle-aged, each wearing bulky wedding rings, and spoke to each other with a bouncy newness that puzzled Max. The woman had long blond hair that matched her necklace and a wrinkle-free face, except for babyish crow's feet that the Botox hadn't yet corrected. Her shoulder-less beige blouse exposed freshly windburned flesh. The man, silver-haired and sweating beneath his blue blazer with gold buttons, spoke as if every syllable were a celebration of his life's conquests, his jaw clenching with potency even in between declarations.

"Sweetheart, hey, excuse me!" He sat up, back erect, and snapped his fingers in the air. "We'd like to order some food."

"Oh my god, don't snap at her," giggled his companion. "That's so rude. Now she's never going to pay attention to us, and I can't say that I blame her."

"I'm sorry, sorry." Callie faced them. "It's nothing personal, sweetheart, just a force of habit from the office with these young guys I've got working for me. You know, working in finance, you'd think making vast sums of money would be enough to keep these boys focused on their work, but now they all have cell phones, and half the time they're taking personal calls at work, if you can believe it."

"It's cool, man, I can take it," replied Callie. "At night, when this place is filled up with out-of-towners, I get my ass slapped probably a dozen times per shift."

"She would like the buffalo wings that your sign mentions."

"With ranch or blue cheese?"

"Oh, I shouldn't be eating anything right now, I SHOULD just wait for dinner!" The woman laughed meaningfully—like something long caught in her heart was finally being purged from her. "See what happened is that I skipped breakfast and lunch because I flew in after him, and we had a dreadful miscommunication about our meetup spot. It's really quite funny now." They grinned at each other.

"Ranch or blue cheese?"

After finishing with the couple, Callie returned to Sam who, somehow emboldened, jabbed for information, which, it occurred to Max, must have been the whole reason they were fumbling away their afternoon in there.

"Nah, never heard of her. Don't think your friend works here," she replied automatically.

"You sure? She was here just last night. Maybe— am I not pronouncing her name right? E-l-e-c-t-r-a." Oddly, Sam slid the signed credit card receipt toward her. "You're *sure*?"

"Shit!" Callie's eyes bulged. "OK, yeah, now I remember her. Listen, she's got the early shift on the upstairs bar tonight—like 9:00. But, guy, please don't get all weird with her and then say I told you she'd be here. That shit happens to girls a lot around here, and it's fucking creepy." Her gray eyes found Max's face, softening a bit.

"How the hell did you persuade her to give you some info," asked Max as they rushed out the door and onto the steamy street.

"I tipped her $100."

Max hurried off alone to the Superdome to watch Atena State's bowl game. They lost badly. Just a little after 9:00pm, he met Sam at BBC, where they remained until nearly dawn. There was no Electra.

2017

In the open atrium beside the offices of the Jackson Construction Company, green Magnolia leaves that had been baked by the July heat into a brittle crunchiness danced recklessly in the thick breeze along the quartz walkway and out onto Commerce Street and the heart of downtown Dallas. Smokers huddled over the cigarette disposal stations set amid the unmanicured dirt tree lot. A DART bus whooshed by, jockeying for its rightful position within the reserved lane where homeward-bound commuters encroached. A trail of over-dressed workers was beginning to trickle out of the old Telecom skyscraper where Jackson Construction and dozens of other firms held offices. It was not even four o'clock, but being a Friday the city was already springing to life. The Downtown Safety Patrol in their yellow vests were surrounding a shirtless vagrant who was screaming incoherently. The police would likely arrive on bicycles soon to escort the gentleman off to—somewhere else.

Inside the trolley car that ran between the downtown commuter rail station and the Oak Cliff neighborhood of south Dallas, the passengers were silent except for two girls who were huddled together over their iPhones. One was short with muscular tanned thighs and the other was tall and pale with tousled Peter Pan hair that was tapered in the back. This taller one was showing her friend a series of text messages.

"You see what Brent sent me? Isn't it funny?"

"Oh, the orange one is Trump, yeah I see it now. So you guys still text?"

"Yeah, I mean he usually sends me memes or like other funny shit he finds online, but yes we talk almost every single day still."

"But like does he text you first?"

"Yeah, oh yeah, I never text him first. Do you see today? He said, 'Good morning, sunshine' and that's what I woke up to this morning." She grinned at her friend.

"But you guys aren't to*gether* together anymore though, right?"

"No, we're just good friends. As in—if he met someone, I'd be happy for him. I would. I would. But— I'd be sad too."

Overhearing this, Max smiled. He always enjoyed when the stains of love were spilled deep enough to withstand the blanching agents of social status. He sat with his knees pressed together beneath a leather messenger bag filled with notebooks and a Jackson Construction-issued laptop.

He hopped off the trolley at the last stop and power

walked down Davis to his apartment building, which was a one hundred-year-old toy factory converted into open-concept, brick-exposed lofts. The bottom floor was exclusively retail, featuring oddities such as a custom ukulele shop and a gong therapy yoga studio. The crown jewel of the building, however, was Accounts Receivable, a grungy old retro-chic bar that was run by the building's owners. There he found his next-door neighbor, Brett, who tended bar on weekends for extra cash.

"Max!" She ran around the length of the bar to give him a greedy hug. The place was empty save for the two of them.

"Hey, Brett! You're here already? It's not even five, how the hell'd you get out of work so early?" Her hair, usually some blond edition, had been artificially dyed back to its natural oaky brown.

"Maximus. I snuck out of work, skipped a staff meeting." She reached for something within her bar station. "I thought I'd get here before Vince comes in and take a couple shift shots so I don't kill myself when the rush comes. You know we have a band tonight—it's total teenybopper trash, so yeah it's going to be an absolute shit show. Do you mind?" She poured herself a double shot glass of Jack Daniels and drank, chasing it with an IPA.

"We're all managing in our own special snowflake ways." They laughed and Brett poured him a cup of orange juice. Producing a wooden spoon and a silver Ziploc sack from his shoulder bag, he meticulously measured and scooped an earthy powder into the cup. Upon making contact with the acidic juice, the ashen mixture coagulated into olive-colored clumps.

"You know, I'm supposed to be doing marketing, like in a professional context, I have a master's degree, for fuck sake. But these Fortune 500 companies see a millennial girl as nothing but a social media maven. They treat me in essence like an intern." Max stirred his concoction. "You have no idea the percentage of my day spent running errands for narcissistic execs. I seriously fetched mockups three times today—like a dog." She leaned over the bar top and squeezed his forearm. "And my boss—I mean my direct supervisor—is a capricious, vindictive ass hole. And all of this, ALL of it would be manageable if they would just throw me a bone and pay a God damn living wage." Max stirred some more.

"Welcome, what can I get for you gentlemen?" Two men in suits and loosened ties walked up to the bar and ordered beers. Max stirred the liquid one final time, noting that the clumps had dissipated into an even emerald juice. He gulped it down, nearly gagging.

"I don't know how you can drink that stuff," said Brett after serving the men. "It makes my heart race, and I get all dizzy and—well—I suppose I can't blame Kratom for the vertigo." She had recently been diagnosed with multiple sclerosis. "OK, but it tastes like death. There's that too."

"Yeah, it's pretty foul. But it helps me focus and be enthusiastic with whatever's in front of me. It's euphoric, but most importantly it's not alcohol."

"I'm not going to lie, sometimes I wish I had known you before you quit drinking. She laughed. "J-K! Kinda."

"Yeah, well, I had a lot of fun—more than the law would allow on a couple occasions. And—I don't want to act like it directly caused my divorce, but it certainly didn't help."

"Um, you're technically still not divorced. But, yeah I get what you mean."

"Right. Let me put it this way: As long as I was going out drinking, I was little more than a liability to those around me. I wasn't—what's the word?— prioritizing the women who actually cared for me."

"And you are now?" She blushed.

At the building gym, Max set the timer to 50 minutes and began jogging increasingly fast, annoyed that the outdated equipment could barely reach his desired pace within the first 30 seconds. He had felt levitated by changing out of his work khakis and into stretchy polyester gym shorts. He was revved up too by the weekend—plans with Sam and the distinct prospect of seeing Brett later in the evening. Thus, he held the up arrow on the machine until it reached a pace of 7.6 mph, which, if he maintained it, would lead him easily to his longtime goal of running a 10k in 50 minutes. By the fifth minute, however, he reduced his speed, and by the time he reached 3 miles, he decided to cut his run short—a 5k would be enough.

Sam met him in his building that night, but seeing the throngs of teenagers camped out with cups of water in their hands and molly in their pockets for the all-ages show, they decided to walk down the street to a cocktail lounge. They stood on the periphery of a large party in the lighted patio. There were black cast-iron tables with citronella candles all around them, but only older couples seemed to sit. Max sipped on black coffee that the bartender had made, wincingly, from a fresh pot. Sam drank an Abita and eyed a group of petite Latinas in the corner. Then, he pulled out his phone:

"I need you to check out this girl's pics. Look. She's, she's attractive, right?"

"Yeah, sure," said Max.

"Look at her arms, though. I can't tell from this one—what with the black and white—if they're kind of big. She's sorta in the background. That's intentional, right? She's definitely hiding something." He scrolled frantically with his thumb. "Here's another one. In her profile pic she seems to have a smokin' hot body, but then look at the others. Look."

"I see, yeah, looks cute enough."

"The rest are just closeups of her face, which appears older now than it did in the first one. That means she's let herself go recently."

"And these are your matches?"

"Yes. Look at this one. She's turned around for Christ's sake so that you can't even see her midsection. I know it sounds shallow, but doesn't it stand to reason that a girl should be at her peak—the pinnacle of her fitness—when she's online trying to meet guys? I mean if she's not going to exert some discipline and get into shape now, then what hope do I have for the future?"

"I think you might need to step back from Tinder for a while. Just to gain some perspective."

"This is all there is. We're thirty-eight years old, probably the oldest ones here—"

"That's not even close to true."

"Whatever. We're getting fucking old, and I can stay in shape, so shouldn't a theoretical woman who's trying to meet dudes online do the same?"

"You're getting a little obsessive with it. I mean it's on the level of—"

"Don't say it."

"Do you not see that you've traded one addiction for another?"

"And you haven't? I saw three cartons of orange juice in your refrigerator and not much else."

"OK, touché. But I'm not wrong about you."

"This is not about her. I haven't—fuck—I haven't even been thinking about her! I don't think about her anymore. I don't. At all."

`Max checked his phone more so to truncate their conversation than out of curiosity, though it had buzzed to life a few times in his pocket. Brett had sent a couple pictures of the crowd back at Accounts Receivable, and she'd also asked a familiar question this time of night to which he didn't deign respond. Then, he did nearly write back when she reminded him of her upcoming surgery and recovery in Houston at the end of August, which would leave her marooned with family and away from him for weeks, maybe all of autumn. Sobriety made the bar seem desolate, an artifice of lights and smiles not dissimilar to a movie set involving actors who all secretly hate one another. Not all bars felt this way to him, in the way that not all dog shelters kill their residents after too much time with no takers.

Meanwhile, Sam appeared to have snagged a taker, as the Latina girls he had been spying were now crawling out of the dim corner and toward the bright patch of patio upon which the men stood beneath a drooping string of orange accent bulbs while leaning with affected ease against a dark table's cold edge.

"Hey, hello, how're you guys doing? I'm Sammie and this is Gabriela." She said her own name with a confident brassy tone, nearly a midwestern twang, but when she said her friend's name, the syllables danced delicately off her tongue with the refined strength of a ballerina.

"Hi, I'm Max, and the dapper gentleman to my right is Sam." They all squeezed hands.

"Um, sorry if we're interrupting your conversation," said Sammie. "You guys did seem *really* into it." She wore a gray Bardot top fringed with white lace, and as she tilted her head up at them and laughed a couple inches of taut skin peeked out from it.

"No, no, we were just talking about—the merits and perils of the digital age," said Sam. He took a long drink from his Abita, finishing the bottle and then clanging it down on the iron table more forcefully than he had intended. Gabriela now regarded him with interest. She was taller and fuller of figure than her friend, but she carried her weight more precariously and kind of shrank into her body in a way that obscured her otherwise athletic build. She wore an asymmetrical white top but sullenly folded her dark arms in front of her like a schoolgirl trapped within the confines of a starched uniform.

"There are merits?" asked Gabriela. She spoke without any trace of an accent, yet there was something about the cadence—a more ancient pacing to the way she spoke.

"Of course! Come on, girl, I couldn't get through my work day without my Instagram feed," said Sammie. She laughed again, and this time Max noticed the glint of a silver belly button ring. A decade ago her outfit would have been called "slutty"—at least on a woman who was nearer to thirty than twenty. In 2017 it was a sobering reminder to men like them of their stolid powerlessness. A welcome change, but a prickly one.

"No, Sammie, you're absolutely right." Gabriela perked up and whipped her head around toward her friend, her green eyes simmering. "We organized the march thanks to social media!"

"Oh, yes!" Unlike Gabriela, Sammie maintained eye contact with the guys, even when she wasn't speaking to them. "We were able to get together for the immigration march around Dallas City Hall. Well, *we* didn't personally organize it, but we mean that everyone was able to put it together and get a really strong turnout in just like three days since it blew up on Facebook and Twitter." Max felt a warm tingling across his left side where Sam was nearby shifting his weight.

"You, ah, I guess are pro-immigration?" Sam's face had taken on a peculiar animation. Gabriela looked askance at the night sky. A fat blur of white light squatted, unblinking, among the firmament above— Mars perhaps. Rarely did the Dallas night sky permit constellations, much less planets, through the film of ambient terrestrial light, but occasionally the heavens revealed themselves in random, chaotic performances. Sammie, visibly exhaling, was about to say something. "I mean, whatever, I don't really know how to feel about it. I suppose illegal immigrants are fine as long as we can secure the border against drug dealers."

"Really, dude?" Sammie had stepped forward toward him. "Who says 'illegal immigrants' anymore? Is it that hard for you to say 'undocumented'? Migrant families seeking work and a safe place to raise their babies are 'illegal' to you?"

"Oh, no, I didn't mean it like that—I mean I didn't vote for Trump or anything, if that's what you think."

"Hey, it looks like you ladies are low on drinks," interrupted Max. "You too, Sam. How about I make a run to the bar?"

"Nah, we're good," said Sammie who motioned to her friend, turning away from the guys.

"OK, um, sorry if I used the wrong term. It's just a word, you know. I mean I'm not advocating for some asinine wall or anything like that." Sam's face was sallow.

"Dude, it's cool, whatever. Gabbie and I gotta get going anyway. Have a nice night." Sammie marched ahead of her friend who lingered a couple steps behind.

"Hey, Sam, I get you," said Gabriela. "It's OK, people say the wrong thing all the time. Sammie's just trying to defend me because I'm—I'm a DACA recipient. It's been really hard on my family, you know? We're living in a state of limbo right now. Just keep that in mind."

"What the hell?" Max turned to Sam after the girls had moved on. "We need to update your vocabulary, man. No one's getting laid these days with fifteen-year-old terminologies."

"That—talk like that—that simpering sensitivity—it makes my fucking blood boil! What moronic affectations these girls have and you—you actually buy that shit. Just words—a person says the wrong fucking word and to that group it's a trigger to unleash their rehearsed faux outrage." Sam had started toward the patio door, which led out to the street, while Max trailed a few steps behind, bogged down by a question: Was Sam's volatility new or just more visible to him through sober eyes? He genuinely tried to solve this riddle until his concentration was broken by another buzz of his phone.

"It's just bull shit because they have the upper hand, and they know it," continued Sam. Probably just Brett, Max reasoned, since he hadn't responded to her earlier invitation. He wanted to see her, he realized, but didn't want to make plans to see her.

"They do? Who, exactly, DACA recipients?"

"Jesus, keep up. No, girls. In an era of apps and one-tap picture enhancing and all that, they know they hold all the advantages—at least at this stage of the game. They're the god damn holy grails and guys like us are disposable." He was only looking over his shoulder, askance, at Max while marching ahead into a dark alleyway detour where he erroneously remembered parking. Max saw that Brett had not in fact pressed her earlier invitation. Did she have another taker? Or, maybe she had only invited him in jest— perhaps her interest had been rendered neutral by their scant (and apparently unsatisfactory!) previous sexual encounters? Either of those possibilities would have chilled him to the bone had he not simultaneously seen the name "Caroline" above a new message.

"Whatever," added Sam. "I might as well head home. This is all pointless anyway. Not a good scene at the bars around here—shitty crowds—like most of Dallas." Max meekly waved goodbye in the direction he thought Sam had started walking down the incorrect black alley and didn't bother amending his friend's path, turning instead toward his own building's golden glow at the end of the block.

Sam's polemic faded into the background space of his mind, blunted and demoted by more joyful considerations. It was a cerebral trick he had perfected during some of Caroline's more caustic invectives, which were those he had earned. He did want to see Brett, he suddenly admitted, but he didn't want to make plans to see her.

Leaning against a column of gray cement and draped about her shoulders in a gossamer beige shawl through which her scapulae poked outwards like horns was Caroline. Her bare leg that popped out from a slit in the front of her charcoal dress was tanned and more rounded than he had remembered from before. She also stood taller, perhaps on account of royal blue Versace pumps with crimson soles. She twisted her mouth wryly at him and with some deliberation stood fully and squared her shoulders, thrusting her bony hands outward in expectation of an embrace. Her eyes wrinkled delicately at the corners as she mimed something approaching a smile, and her forehead glistened evenly like the hood of a car that's been buffed to a glossy perfection. Various metallic parts jangled around her neck and wrists, but the fingers on her left hand, he noticed, remained free. Thus, he felt safe in asking: "So, did Lord Carrot finally pop the question? I assume you're here to ask in person for a divorce."

"You're funny. Always so funny." She wasn't laughing. Her nose, always a svelte Greek form, was somehow more delicate now, like a porcelain doll's. This was for him, Max reasoned, these expensive modifications (or commodification, he thought bitterly, before feeling a surge of guilt). She had invested in herself, hedged her bets against him—or, put another way, had culled from herself a look that was meant for someone better than him. "No, he did not. And you know that's not his name. His name is Lorne Caron, not that it matters."

"Whatever, it's some ass hole British aristocrat name."

"He's Canadian. But I don't want to talk about him any more than you do. In fact, we broke up. And no, I'm not here to drop bombshells on you, which I'm sure is going to be your next snide comment. If you were on social media, you would already know all this. I've been very up front about it. Also—" she paused, and her shoulders seemed to soften a bit. "My dad died."

"Good." Max said it automatically before he could craft a more nuanced response. "I mean, that is good, right? Or—"

"Are you kidding? Absolutely! It's a fucking celebration." She was looking away from him, off somewhere into the past. Her face didn't hold within it the springiness of a smile, yet something had begun to thaw. "But, I don't want to talk about him either."

He unlocked the door, and Caroline squirmed past him, unprompted, plopping herself down on the couch and flinging her shoes off. "Huh, it's not as disgusting as I expected. Care for a glass of chardonnay?" She had been toting a wine bottle under her arm.

"No, thanks. You of all people should remember that I don't drink—anymore."

"Oh, right, yes." She paused. "Still? I figured that wouldn't last once you were single. Huh, it just goes to show. . . " She trailed off, dreamily. Well, mind if I pour a glass or two? Is that going to tempt you?"

"Let me open that for you."

"It's funny y'know how God damn obstinate you were when I desperately wanted you to stop. Begged, pleaded, cursed, all that—couldn't get through to you. I never drank with you, not after your DUI anyway. But now, now that I've discovered that fuck—" She sighed and sank triumphantly into his couch with her filled glass, the golden strands of her asymmetrical bob splashing across the emerald leather. Without making eye contact she hoisted an open hand and waved him over. "—fuck, I love a nice chardonnay. Of course, just my luck that now, NOW is when you won't drink."

"Had a few already I take it." He sniffed the bottle, enjoying for a moment the tannic acid before clanking it down onto the white granite counter.

"Oh, that's rich, real funny—you should know how a drunky acts. I had one bottle, give or take, but I Ubered over here. You see, I didn't drive, sweets."

"You know what? You use the word 'funny' more than anyone I've ever met, yet you never laugh." By the time he flicked on the TV (selecting a music channel that played tunes from the early 2000s) and made his way to the couch, her glass was empty.

"Because life isn't funny, Max. Try living my life for a few days. Try it! Oh, I'd love to see you making home visits to diseased old curmudgeons that decades ago were written off by their families—and usually with good reason: stole from their sons, molested their daughters, filled their kids' childhoods with the screams of their battered mothers. Then these old fucks still, STILL have it in them to grab my ass and call me all sorts of pretty little names like 'Sugar Tits' or worse. Meanwhile they're living on a fixed income of $600 a month and their meds cost half of that, and of course they can't walk up steps anymore, so now they need an $8000 AmeriGlide Platinum Curved Stair Lift to navigate up their weird ass decrepit stairways, and I get to fill out reems of paperwork to encourage the state to purchase it for them. Those are the easiest cases. The really hard ones, and this is most of them, are the sweetest people who just happen to be desperately poor because they made the embarrassing miscalculation of living too long after entering retirement. For those little old angels, I buy groceries out of my own pocket and deliver them after work hours. Then, Max, do you know what happens just after I get to know them and actually look forward to seeing them when I wake up in the morning and get ready to drive to my shitty job?" With sober deliberation she placed her glass on an end table and wiped the back of her hand across her eyes. They faced each other finally on the couch, and Max, having brought the bottle with him, refilled her glass before answering.

"They die, Caroline."

"Yes, Max, they die. It's fucking heartbreaking." She was resisting a full sob but buoyed by a long gulp of chardonnay.

"I know it is. And, I know it destroys you every time. We've had this conversation, Caroline. Countless times. I'm not saying that to be glib or—callous or—whatever it is you think of me these days. I'm just saying that so that you know that I've been listening to you all these years. I know what you've been feeling all along—know it by heart."

"No, sweetie, you don't know. You've always thought of me as this hateful troll that bitches at you about drinking or hanging out with Sam in New Orleans or whatever, but that's just because I saw you destroying your body the way those poor old people had, and I was constantly afraid that you too were going to just die someday out of the blue." She was visibly resisting another surge of sobs pulsing through her body. "And what would have happened to you and Sam if all his stalking would have paid off and he would have gotten together with Electra? I actually knew her, albeit briefly, and she was the biggest God damn train wreck of us all. She was coked out of her mind whenever she was working, and during her breaks between sifts she would do shots in the back with the manager. The rare times when I saw her sober, she was the meanest bitch you'll ever meet. I guess she was pretty in a grungy sort of way, but her eyes were always bloodshot and puffy, and half the time she was bruised purple from whatever drug-dealer boyfriend at the time was slapping her around. I wanted to escape all that. It wasn't just Katrina that kept me from returning to that city. Somehow, though, you two saw her as this mythic creature—like a nymph or something—and if I tried to correct that image, you just thought I was being a bitch."

"I never blamed you for leaving me. I kept making mistakes, and by the time we moved back here and I sobered up, it was too late—the happiness ledger was too far in the red. When you moved out to get your own place and sort things out, I naively thought it was a positive step forward, a chance to reboot. It was when you found a sugar daddy that I stopped wanting to casually share pleasantries with you over text. Forgive me."

"Oh, there it is." She poured herself a glass and crossed her legs, her narrow chin jutting outward. "You get to cheat—what was it: once, twice, maybe other times that I didn't know about? But, God forbid I have a life after we have clearly split up. Yeah, Lorne's loaded, but that isn't what attracted me to him. I didn't ask him to save me or take care of me. He insisted. I had planned to keep working, but he saw the toll it was taking on me and—and he thought I needed a break from all that."

"We were, you and I, still thinking about going back to counseling when you announced that you had moved in with this douche."

"Well what was I supposed to do?" Her fingers swiping at her cheeks could no longer keep pace with the stream of hot tears that seemed to be manufactured by an exothermic combination of anger and heartbreak. "I was on the verge of defaulting on my student loans, I was miserably unhappy at work, and I had long since lost faith in us. Then, Lorne just offered to solve all of those problems for me. I thought maybe he loved me and just saw how much I was struggling and wanted to share his—his good luck with me. I know now how foolish I was. But what was I supposed to do? What other options did I have? Was I supposed to get a second or third job to make ends meet?" He thought about Brett on the other side of the wall—or maybe she was still behind the bar.

"You know, when a person is disgustingly rich, he can just keep on spending money on interesting things until the hangers-on around him forget that he isn't actually interesting himself."

"I know that now. But it doesn't matter what you know when you're weeks behind on all your payments, when every month the electric bill arrives in that special pink envelope instead the white one. And, yes, he did have 'hangers-on' (as you so condescendingly put it), but that wasn't me. It wasn't! I mean, look at us!"

"No. No, it wasn't." Max turned away from her and slithered over to the window. It was so highly placed that any view of the city was inaccessible for someone of Max's average height. He had to thrust himself upward onto his toes before the glowing green outline of the Bank of America Plaza building, which dominated the downtown Dallas skyline, graced his view. "You're right," he said after some time. "You tried your best to stay with me, and I treated you terribly." He joined her on the couch, as Caroline smacked away a final trickle of tears and smiled at him. She fumbled her wine glass down onto the end table, causing it to fall and spill a few slow drops like blood from a wound whose itchy scab has been pealed a moment too soon. She kissed him, probingly at first, exploratory, and then hiked the hem of her dress, freeing her legs to bend and straddle his lap. Then she showered him with kisses that were sloppy but met fully by his own enthusiastic response, their bodies soon clawing at each other and writhing with wild abandon.

Caroline was still asleep in the calm early Saturday morning hours before the sun fully illuminated the bedroom portion of the old loft. Max had awoken with a shudder, feeling the sting of some unseen anxiety, prompting him to snatch his phone from his jeans, which were still crumpled inside out by the couch, and head to the bathroom. Before he left, though, he lifted a sheet and gently placed it over Caroline's naked body. Under the early stirrings of morning light her bronze face revealed lines he had never before noticed, creases that refused to be filled even by clumps of foundation that had dried overnight like crumbly, stale bread.

Within the privacy of the bathroom, the only room with a door, Max checked his phone. There was a message from Brett:

"OK dude I get it, you don't owe me anything at all. We're not a couple and you're free to fuck whoever you want. But seriously, I'm not even worthy of a response after I invite you over?! Instead, you have loud sex with your ex-wife, at least I assume that's who that was. She came to the bar while I was working and introduced herself and asked for your apartment number. It's one thing for you to date someone but rubbing it in my face that you aren't interested in me is pretty shitty, man."

* * *

Sam had stopped going to work. He called his friends throughout the first three days to see who else could go out at night, claiming that Mortimer, Vale, and Associates (the Dallas-based capital management firm where he worked as a programmer) was in the midst of a summer lull and wouldn't miss him. On the fourth day he went dark—no texts or tweets except to cryptically announce on his social media "The Crescent City" with a picture of a moonlit river and no further explanation. Max called him on the fifth day and confirmed that, yes, he had flown down to New Orleans, but he spoke only in nostalgic turns, noting where this and that used to be on Bourbon Street and what whitewashed reboot had replaced it. He didn't need to say that this would be his last trip, just like he hadn't needed to ask Max to join him. Sam was utterly non-responsive on the sixth day, posting nothing and ignoring incoming messages. When Max began calling him, he didn't answer until the third try, and then without so much as a greeting he plunged into a chance encounter:

"Do you remember Carlos? Yes you do. He managed that disgusting smoke-filled riverboat bar by the casino—Slick Rick's. Anyway, he's friends with Electra—or was when I ran into him a year ago. I had seen her just a couple years before and I think—I almost think they had dated at some point in the past. So, I went in there today, and he doesn't work there anymore, but the place is populated with idiots who all claim to know where he is now. So, you there?"

"Yes."

"Yeah, so a couple of them told me he's now bartending at some dive bar in the Marigny, and I Ubered over there to see but of course he wasn't working today. God damn it!" Sam's slippery links to the past were beginning slide from his grasp.

"Hey, let's hangout when you get back. When are you flying to Dallas?"

"Tomorrow. Wish I had one more day. Damn it all!" He hung up.

Then, on the seventh day, when Sam was supposed to have resurrected himself back in Texas but had again gone ominously dark, Max drove to his apartment.

After texts, calls, knocks, shouts, and all other such entreaties went unanswered, he tried the knob and found that it turned freely. This was not a positive development, as Max had never known Sam to have left his door unlocked. He could be careless with himself, but he never trusted his life to the hands of others—with one exception. The door silently gave way, meaning the alarm had not been set. And, in an instant, as Max peeked around the frame, he knew why. A face that had once belonged to Sam greeted him—with ashen skin with a mouth scrunched into a voiceless scream below eternal, unblinking eyes that bulged past the orbital bones as if they had outgrown their own delicate humanity. His feet did not touch the floor, and around his neck he wore a coil of ivory rope.

Max must have called 9-1-1 before blacking out because his next memory was Brett picking him up from the hospital. She had called herself "Mrs. Orbach" to the ER nurse and played the role well. She fed him pills according to the doctor's recommendation and wordlessly drove him home. He was already drifting off when she slung him into his bed and draped a sheet over him. His eyes were closed, his breathing heavy, and though he was still clawing at the final strands of consciousness within him, he must have appeared dead asleep. The final thoughts that fluttered across the embers of his waking mind were the books strewn across Sam's coffee table: *The Sun Also Rises* and David Foster Wallace's *Infinite Jest*. There was also *The Great Gatsby*, which had been opened to the inscription, "ONCE AGAIN TO ZELDA," though "Zelda" had been scratched out. The books were not clutter or a carelessly scattered mess, as they would have seemed to anyone else. Rather, he had arranged them as a form of collective note, which was apparent to Max when he considered the meticulously simple order of the other items in the apartment. He tried to analyze it but found his mind too gooey to be of any use. Then he felt what must have been a kiss on his forehead, and he tried to mouth a response with his own lips but found them paralyzed. As the blackness of the void washed fully over him, his final waking moment was filled by a sweet voice saying, "God, I wish you knew I loved you."

* * *

A few days passed and summer yawned toward late August. His phone had died in the night, which he perceived as a mercy kill. It lay serenely within a pocket of some sweaty jeans, safely silent. The morning light stabbed past gaps in the curtains that were always ill-shaped for the broad awning window that sat, tauntingly immutable, having been soldered shut in the 50s after an industrial accident had destroyed a few laborers. That's always the case, Max thought: People die in all sorts of gruesome ways and then the rest of us seal things up. If he climbed up the brick wall to that wide iron mouth and bashed it open with a hammer and poked his head out into the wind, what would he see? Paved ground, three floors below? Sure, but it wouldn't be the same view as through secured glass. With the naked eye he would see his own mortality, a corpse landing strip. And, that view is what we protect ourselves against more than the fall itself. What did those immigrant carpenters think while freefalling to their deaths after a scrap heap caught sparks from a blow torch and exploded a tank of liquid chemicals, launching them up from their kneeling postures and out that window? A window jacked open, no doubt, so that assembly line zombies didn't pass out from noxious fumes and would keep on their feet for a few more years until the mesothelioma got them. Did they pray in Mandarin or Spanish? Or did they bask in their elevation, their exit? An exit now blocked by dollops of silicone caulk. No more lost productivity. It was an arrogant thought, one mercifully cut off by a knock.

"Max?" The figure who spoke resembled Caroline so nearly that it must have been her in one iteration or another. Her cheeks were sunken or might have just appeared that way by contrast to the bulging flesh that resembled wet tea bags beneath her eyes. Sleeping in Lord Carrot's guest house must not be agreeing with her, he thought. It wasn't a wish, merely a robotic observation. Besides the weariness etched in her face, though, she was accoutered in measured brilliance—a black pant suit that looked new. Christ, Lord Carrot must have bought her an outfit for every occasion before casting her out of the big house. How disappointing for him that no misfortune befell any of his associations in time for him to see how her figure filled out her mourning wear.

"Max, I brought something, brought this for you," she stammered. "It's a lamb roast I made last night, and I thought maybe it would help you out, maybe give you lunch." Caroline never cooked. Max accepted the Pyrex dish and managed to whisk aside his skepticism, inviting her in. Still, she seemed audacious with her clingy black outfit and faded emerald stone necklace— at least for this time of the morning, if indeed it was still morning. He truly did not know. Her hair had been scorched from its golden glean to nearly copper. With Lord Carrot's financial spigot squeezed off, she had tried herself to touch up her color from a box. He knew this because while they were together, she almost always used a box, and it never quite came out right. Reminding himself of this was supposed to help, but he just couldn't feel anger toward her anymore.

She accepted his invitation, but before entering the apartment a third face appeared in the hallway.

"You must be Caroline," said Brett. She stepped out into the hallway wearing Winnie the Pooh adult onesie pajamas at which Max chuckled, forgetting himself for a moment. "I don't believe we've met, officially I mean."

"Oh, the bartender!" Caroline was still facing Max. "Shit, that's so rude. Sorry, sweetie, you have a name." Caroline pivoted, towering (in her heels) over the barefoot other woman. "Oh, don't tell me—you served me a drink once here before—it's Brittney—or no— Britt, right?" She smiled and extended her bony hand. With her other hand she dumped the warm dish into Max's hands and straightened the bangs that framed her face.

"It's Brett actually, but that's really not important." She accepted the outstretched hand and smiled with a tilt to her head that Max couldn't quite understand, but he loved how her untamed brunette curls bounced unpredictably atop her head and past her shoulders. He was trying to remember which gentle dog breed she resembled, but the thought was severed by a hoot from Caroline.

"Ah, I almost fuhgot!" She spoke with the non-rhotic *r*—a remnant of her New Orleans accent that poked out in times of stress. "Hun, we all want to thank you so much for driving him home from the hospital the other day. I spoke to his parents on the phone, and we're all just so thankful that he has reliable friends. I used to be his emergency contact for the longest time, but, well, you know. He was actually on my insurance for most of the time we've been back in Texas—up until recently when he finally found that job at Johnson Construction."

"Jackson," snapped Brett.

"Excuse me?"

"He works for Jackson Construction, not Johnson."

"She's right," said Max. "And Brett works in marketing. She only bartends downstairs on the weekends."

"You know," began Caroline, "it's getting awfully close to lunchtime." She examined Brett's cartoon pajamas, then turned to Max. "You want me to come in and heat this up for you now?"

"It's terribly sweet of you to bring this for me, Caroline, but—" He glanced back and forth at both women. "I'm just not ready for lunch."

That afternoon, well after Caroline had departed, Brett appeared at his door. She was dressed for work, which didn't mean much for bartenders at Accounts Receivable except that her hair had been tamed by a golden hair clip with shimmery green stones, and her pajamas had been swapped for a white blouse and distressed blue denim jeans. She squeezed his hand and led him to the couch.

"Maximus!" She smiled brightly before a heaviness overtook the buoyancy of her eyes.

"Brett, aren't you supposed to be at work soon? I was planning on stopping by to see you before I go out tonight."

"Oh? Going out?"

"By myself, just to the old coffee shop. I need to get out, you know?"

"Yeah, I get it, dude. Totally understandable." And then: "All right, Max, I do have to be at work in a few minutes, but first—I—I want to talk to you about Caroline." Her right hand was clasping her left wrist and only partially masking a persistent tremor.

"Yeah, sorry if she seemed a bit rude today. She has a way of being a little—"

"No, that's not—that's not what's important to me. I just want to say one thing, or rather two things, if I'm being honest. And, the first point is this: Make sure you two know what you're doing if you're going to get back together. You're both—seeking something at the moment—"

"Jesus, story of my life."

"And when two seekers cross paths it can sometimes erroneously feel like they are each other's Shangri-La, when in reality they are just lost and happened to bump into each other. Does that make sense?"

"Yeah, but Brett, listen—"

"No, Max, let me finish. That was just the first half of what I wanted to say, and I needed to say that part to be at least somewhat at peace with this next bit. Here it goes." She sighed and rose up off the couch, turning away from him. "Caroline is still your wife. Or, what I mean is there must be a reason you two never officially divorced. It's been years of separate apartments and even a serious boyfriend, and yet when it all comes down to it and the shit hits the fan, she's there for you. You've always been a bit aloof with me—ignoring texts and whatnot—and I suppose I've looked past that since you could also sit for hours on end at the bar sipping on water and keeping me company during my shifts or bringing me food while I was working. But, lately you've somehow become even less responsive to me, and that would be OK, just you being you, except that I have the sinking suspicion that she's the one distracting you. So, I get it. It seems that you two have an opportunity to rekindle things now that she's available, and you should go for it, I guess, if that's what you want. I'll be fine." She had backed herself up against the door and even began fiddling with the handle. "Don't blindly attach yourself to someone else's dream." She paused, before quietly adding, "again."

"Brett, what if—"

"No." He was pursuing her across the open living room/kitchen area that all bled together into one big concrete void before the door. "Don't say anything, Max. Not right now, anyway, while everything's so raw. Just—you do you. Take care of yourself." And she was gone.

* * *

Max sat amid the striped shade of the brass balustrade by the moonlit corner window of the Oak Cliff coffee shop in a dark nook of south Dallas that hadn't yet been swallowed up by the tsunami of gentrification across the neighborhood. It wasn't really a coffee shop. Truly it was more of a bar that served coffee and croissants well into the night, even while local jazz combos blasted their horns and clacked the snare drum's rim. A few old-timers also drank lukewarm coffee and nibbled on pastries around chessboards, but usually by sundown the mood had shifted, as green bottles of cheap lager clanged across the laminated table tops. It was the kind of place their grandfathers would have recognized—except for the craft beer options that were beginning to spread across the taps. Max had begun drinking coffee there on those late nights when he sought anonymity. A year ago he was the only white face. While still in the minority, their numbers were growing each week, spreading their taste and money within the black-owned business. Still, Max was the only one who sat alone. So, it surprised him when a man passed by the row of vacant barstools and plopped down next him.

"Sup man? Whatch you doin hidin' out in the corner sippin' on old Frank's shitty coffee?" Max wasn't eager to engage, but he turned to him and was—impressed. The interloper wore a wisteria purple fedora and matching satin vest, both of which complemented a thin moustache atop a dark face. His pants were jet black and almost as glossy as his polished loafers that glistened from a brass buckle. Despite the layers of clothing, he appeared at peace with the August heat. His face was an even-toned matte shade of espresso, not like Max's that had been moistened and painted a splotchy red by an angry sun on the walk over. This guy, though, didn't seem like he could have even existed in the daylight.

"Frank? That the owner's name? I've been coming here for months now, but I guess I never had the pleasure." Max felt the swollen, sagging weight of his phone burning in his pocket like a baby's simmering potentiality. He wondered when social graces would permit him to dig it out. Not yet. This guy had that type

of barbed intensity like the infirmed or intoxicated—
though he was neither.

"Fuckin Frank." He said it with a lifted tone that
wasn't quite a question and even less a declaration.
"You've seen him. Drank his liquor and shitty coffee.
Probably talked to him a time or two if you been
haunting this place as you say. No way around it. He's
always behind the bar—there right now as a matter of
fact. And—if he sees a white boy like you he's going to
talk—figures you and your friends got spending
money."

"Well then you're both wrong. I've never had his
liquor, and I don't have any money. I don't drink—
anymore." He sipped his coffee and realized that it was,
in fact, quite bad. "Thus, the shitty coffee." Was that his
phone humming against his thigh, or was it merely
some caffeine-induced fasciculation?

"No shit? Don't drink? I know there's a story
behind this. Come on, man, unburden thy sins to
Reggie. For with the heart man believeth unto
righteousness; and with the mouth confession is made
unto salvation!" He swallowed the remnants of amber
liquor in a whiskey tumbler with that effortless
affectation of movie mobsters. He could have hoisted a
Tommy Gun and scattered bullets across the wood-
paneled walls and it wouldn't have surprised Max.
Instead, he flung an ivory smile at a group of pretty
women who were receptive targets. By the time they
were smiling back he had already ducked back toward
his companion—a trick that intrigued them.

"Reggie, is it? I'm Max. And, your New Testament
shamanism has no effect on me. I'm Jewish."

"Maximillian, Holy Roman Emperor! I speak from

the book of Reginald, for I have appropriated white Christian culture for the Marxist Negro agenda." He looked like he believed it too.

A group of attractive middle-aged women with bright red lipstick and active eyes squeezed by the bar and managed to bounce quick looks at the dark-complexioned specimen owning a stool—and second looks at his hunched white sidekick. Reggie had the eerie ability to fold them into his field of view without turning away from his male companion. That seemed to be his way, everything bending to the centripetal force of his gravitational will. One of the women, the most attractive and most taken, sort of leaned toward him and accelerated as she flew past him, her comet-like ring shimmering atop her left hand. For his part, Reggie nodded toward her, if it were indeed a nod, and casually warmed the room with his fiery gaze. Max felt something bubbling within his pocket and this time was certain of its silicon origins. For some reason he thought of Caroline.

"Maximillian, now I'm going to buy you a drink. If you don't want it, we'll send it over to one of those lovely ebony ladies, and I won't mind one bit the conversation that will follow. But, if you are so inclined, I suspect locked within that nice white Jewish boy exterior are some stories I want to hear." Max's hand, which had lain upon his pants pocket, thumbing the comforting rectangular contour below, now lifted up to the bar top, as he squared his shoulders and mimicked the posture of his companion. Could it have been Brett who texted? Outside, the streetlights glowed greenish yellow in the foreground of the hazy black, starless sky. Pedestrians, now a continuous flow, orbited around the block with a confident chorus of voices—some singing along with the silent music of their minds while others heckled and teased one another with reedy shouts of laughter.

"I'm an alcoholic, Reginald. That's the story. And now you want to dangle the offer of a drink in front of me? Better send it on down the bar." Max rose and whisked a few stubborn strands of hair away from his sticky forehead. "It was nice talking to you, man, but I gotta go. Can't jeopardize my sobriety on a random night out in Oak Cliff." He reached out a hand toward Reggie, who hadn't budged. A jazz trio began warming up on the far side of the room where, rather than a stage, there was a small nook cleared by shoving aside a couple tables. The upright bass player began a splashy, walking line that bounced off the walls. The low sting of cheap whiskey pinched their noses as Frank poured freely across a row of shot glasses, much of the liquor dripping down the sides into golden puddles on the bar top.

"Sit down," said Reggie, unsmiling" and still refusing Max's outstretched hand. "That ain't a story."

"Huh? What's not?"

"Calling yourself an alcoholic is not a story, it's a label—and a cheap one at that. You do know that I see white folks come in here all the time, and typically I don't exert myself trying to make their acquaintance. But you, you're different. Always by yourself just sitting there in the corner. I've never before known a white dude who actually looks at black people and white people with the same exact expression on your face, just this quiet, hollow stare. Now, I want to know why that is. I want to know your story and why you don't act like all the corny motherfuckers who come in here with their retro frames and ironic t-shirts. Hordes of them. Comin' in here spoutin' off to one another about the history of the place, how it was founded a hundred years ago as a safe haven for black blues musicians who weren't big enough for Deep Ellum or white enough for anywhere else in Dallas."

"Is all that true?" Max dropped down onto his stool.

"Hell yeah. But that's not the point. The point, Max, is that this is a real mother fuckin place with actual black folks who still enjoy it in the present. Some of us aren't ready to become an amusement park where bearded white dudes with trust funds show off for their skinny ass girlfriends. You ain't like all of them other gentrifying mother fuckers—pretending to like jazz and shit. As a matter of God damn fact (and I do like the flavor of a fat, juicy fact) I'm starting to think you come here to escape from all that. So, Emperor Maximillian, I asked you for a story, and unless I'm reading you all wrong, you're the type of dude that doesn't really talk until you have a drink in front of you. Tell me I'm wrong."

"OK. All right. Fuck it, let's get some liquor and talk." Reggie signaled to Frank. "Here's the basic plot: I moved to Brooklyn a few years back with my wife. Didn't know anyone, so I hung around bars a lot by myself until I made a couple friends. One night, after I'd been drinking beer and watching a basketball game with these guys at their apartment in Queens, I tried to take the 7-train home, but it was running with massive delays, and finally I gave up on it. Turned away from the platform, ran down the stairs and out to the street to see if there were any Borough Cabs out there, but of course there weren't any. Are you familiar with New York City, Reggie?" He nodded, his face handsomely illuminated by the citrusy glow of the moonlight that flooded through the window.

"This was before ride-sharing apps, so my only option was to climb back up to that cold platform and wait for the damn 7-train. The problem, though, is that Caroline, that's my wife, had been blowing up my phone for the last hour—see, she didn't much care for the fact that I'd found some drinking buddies, and I'd already breached my curfew." Frank had slid two glasses of straight whiskey in front of them, and Max realized that he had unconsciously begun to drink already. He wasn't sure if the budding ruddiness around his cheeks was a symptom of the alcohol or a ghostly residual agitation. "Anyway, I was pretty hammered, but I kept getting bitched at, so I finally found my car parked on the street by this dude's apartment and started home. Well, I had only been in New York for a couple months at that point and didn't know the roads very well. Got lost in some wayward Queens neighborhood (they all look familiar until they don't), turned the wrong way on a one-way street and got pulled over. So, after a DUI and then a couple drunken nights dabbling with cheating, I gave up alcohol for good. At first my temperance was court-ordered, but then I completed a treatment program and flew to New Orleans to meet an old friend. As a last-ditch attempt to save my marriage after that, I chose to give it up— declared myself an alcoholic."

"And did that work?" Reggie was slurping his whiskey like a child with a sippy cup. He signaled again to Frank.

"Huh?"

"Did your newfound teetotalling ways save your marriage?"

"Um, no I guess not. We separated right after that and have been apart ever since. We each ended up moving back to Texas, but up until recently she's been living with some boyfriend."

"I see." Reggie just stared at him for a second and finished his glass. He drank liquor without flinching the way chiseled action flick heroes did. The tenor saxophone's masculine bellowing screeched up into a desperate upper altissimo range. "So then, Maximillian," he said, clearing both of their empty glasses and positioning in front of them two newly filled shot glasses, "it sounds to me like you've got a woman problem more than a drinking problem." He was a character straight out of Chuck Palahniuk, Max thought. Abruptly, Reggie stood and dropped some cash on the bar. "Drink your shot so we can go. You and me are gonna take a little walk so I can hear more of this here tale. See, now you've piqued my curiosity, but you still haven't told me the real story—the one I care about. I wanna know about the part that came before all this, the part where you learned to drink and pick up women—the juicy shit. Maybe you took all that too far in the end, but that's still what made the man."

Everyone on the street seemed to recognize Reggie the man, but what they also managed to read was an imperceptible something within his face that told them not stop him and chat—that he was preoccupied. He was an active and animated listener, his cues serving as guides rather than reactions, while Max regaled him with the decade-long series of nights wandering the French Quarter, like a moth trailing a light that has since been extinguished. Reggie sort of pushed him through the tale, coloring in the black spots of Max's memory. As an audience, he was placid, respectful but hardly passive. Max couldn't imagine him remaining passive in any situation, while it suddenly occurred to him that he, himself, had been nothing but passive up to this point in his life.

"So, I get what this Sam cat was after: the white whale," began Reggie as they continued toward the darker end of the block, "but what you still haven't said is what you got out of the whole deal."

"White whale? That's a hell of a thing to call a woman." Max was feeling a bit drunk, the old vigor returning but his tolerance emaciated.

"Come on, man. This been your whole life? Deflecting real shit with humor? Talk to Reggie and tell me why you tagged along with Captain Ahab for his reckless pursuit."

"That's funny actually because more than once I called him Captain Ahab while we were driving across Louisiana. The truth, though, I guess is that I don't know why I went along with it."

"Yeah you do. Just say it."

"OK, OK, let me really think and try to answer your question." They had drunk cheap beers at two more bars along their path down the street, which was moving away from the part of the neighborhood Max knew. He genuinely tried to focus his mind but found memories and feelings to be dissociated pieces that had shattered apart and couldn't easily be paired up again.

"I didn't ask you a question. See, I already know

the truth, but I want to hear you say it. Is it a problem for you to say it?"

"No, but—I just, I really don't know how to answer, err, explain what I mean—"

"Listen, it's cool, Max. Let me help you out with that. There's one more bar I want to take you to." They turned south on a street called "Carmichael Way." Max had never heard of that road nor had he been that far south into Oak Cliff. In fact, his explorations had always before terminated blocks earlier. Through the warm cocoon of alcohol swirling around him, he began to feel something else.

"Um, Reggie, I'm no tour guide, but this street's pretty dark. I don't think there're any bars down this way."

"Sure there are, Max. There's always been some haunts down this way. They just ain't the kind of joints you ever bothered to check out. Come on, man. Don't be scared of some black folks."

They plodded down the dimly lit path that seemed more of an alleyway than a bona fide street. There were, in fact, streetlamps punctuating the cracked sidewalk, but either the city didn't deign to light them in this part of town or else they needed repairs. In any case, only the moonlight offered just enough white light to illuminate the hand-painted signs of businesses that peaked out above untamed bushes on rusted iron posts. Yes, once Max's eyes adjusted to the deficit of light, he noticed a proud procession of family industries along Carmichael that quietly persisted under lunar slumber, darkened until yawning open before dawn. These places had names like J&J's Body Shop, Khan and Sons Plumbers, and Gutierrez Dresses and Tailor. They reminded him of the work crews in New Orleans that would come out at dawn to repair the city, patch it up, wash away the sticky filth left by the careless hands of nighttime revelers who only relinquished control when they collapsed onto starched white down pillows of hotel rooms throughout the Quarter.

As they neared an intersection, the only blip of light ahead came from a DART bus that was at capacity, a sight Max had never seen in years of Dallas living. Where could all those folks be heading at this time of night? As the thought hit him, the bus vanished from his frame of view and revealed—something else. Sure enough, just as Reggie had said, there was a bustling scene up ahead. The bar, if you could call it that, was more of an open grassy lot fenced in by a ramshackle split rail fence made of cedar logs. Within the yard were probably a dozen carousers, some with cans of cheap beer, others smoking cigarettes, and a few just laughing and shouting greetings to one another. A plume of whiteness floated upward from an enormous black smoker, spreading the peppery scent of marbled brisket brushed with a Texas dry rub that released a tangy spiciness. In the background was a pale cinderblock building that served as the main bar, yet they found few patrons inside—solely a pretty, middle-aged bartender who was perched on a stool next to the gray-bearded face of a man with a "Vietnam Veterans" baseball cap. There was a pedestal-stand fan oscillating in the corner, a bulky compact disc jukebox, and a pool table with fresh green felt that was nearly pressed up into the corner. The door was propped open by an enormous rock and the buoyant shouts from the front patio outshined the wan tune buzzing out of the speakers. The Texas summer night had reached the habitable point when the temperature dropped below 80 for a few hours.

"Reggie baby!" said the bartender. "You brought a white boy." They hugged and the man in the cap stood up to shake his hand.

"What's up, Sheila? How you gonna keep these old dogs off when you lookin' all stunning in that dress?" He accepted her outstretched hand and knowingly flipped it over and kissed her palm. Then, to the man: "How you doing, Uncle Joe?"

"Reginald! Sit down and have a drink with your uncle."

"You sure do like to collect them," said Sheila, eyeing Max. Her face was firm, ageless in its resilient lines and polished onyx exterior, her eyes the same emerald green of Max's. She held enough youthful pluckiness to bate the younger men who came at her with narrowed eyes and crisp stacks of cash but also the granite resilience to spurn them with motherly tenderness. She kept an eye on Max in that searching way that could have seemed predatory had it not been spiked with an air of sympathy.

"Uncle Joe, let's work on that bottle of Jack you been drinking from. Sheila, I'll buy the bottle and pour us some shots. You too pretty to work, sit down, please. Then we'll take the bottle outside to the corner and pour one out for Trey."

"I'm not supposed to let him take the bottle outside, you know," she said to Max. "If it were anyone else in the world, I wouldn't." He knew she meant it too. Reggie filled three glasses with the pungent amber liquor and then sampled his as if it were a glass of fine wine. He made similar gestures with all moments of his life, as far as Max could tell.

They drank. Reggie distilled for his uncle the many years of Max's New Orleans sojourns into a few tight sentences that rang with a note of—was it sarcasm? Not quite, but there was a new tone that pealed forth from his companion that Max hadn't heard until the present audience. After finishing their glasses, Reggie clutched the half-spent bottle and led the other men outside. Sheila, who had been sanitizing stained glasses behind the bar, sighed and stared with arms folded.

"Uncle Joe, you wanna do the honors?" They were standing past the wooden fence atop the dark, pockmarked pavement. Reggie looked down and offered the bottle to the older man.

"Nah, nah, I've done enough of that in my lifetime. It's time for you younger guys to fight the good fight. Besides, I know you, Reginald. You were as close to Little Joe as anyone, and you know you've always been another son to me."

"This for you, Trey," said Reggie, splashing onto the black pavement liquor that looked flesh-colored in the pale lamplight coloring the street. He passed the bottle around so that each man could drink—atheists' communion, Max thought to himself, before feeling silly and relieved that he hadn't said it aloud. "Gone before your time. Shoulda been makin' a life for yourself right about now, but they gunned you down."

"He was murdered?" Max spoke only a moment before realizing that there could have been no other way.

"The psychos shot him seven times," said Uncle Joe. "In the back."

"Gotta stay clear of those animals, only way to stay alive. They're predators in this community, hunting us down." He passed the bottle to Max. "Your turn. You wanna pour one out for your man?"

"So—was your cousin involved in some gang activity or something like that, Reggie?"

"What!?" barked Uncle Joe. "Hell no!"

"Max, do you assume that every gunned down black man deserved what he got because he was caught up in some criminal enterprise?" Reggie cocked his head, more satisfied than angry, like a teacher who's just ensnared the class clown.

"I didn't mean—I'm sorry—I was just guessing that because you said—"

"Oh I know what you were doing, Emperor Maximillian. Us black folks use words like 'psychos' and 'animals' and that means one thing to your tribe and something entirely different to this neighborhood. We weren't talking about some fuckin' gang bangers."

"Look, I didn't mean any harm—"

"I know you didn't *mean* any harm, Max. Listen, it's time now for me to tell you a story—a story that starts off over in your part of Oak Cliff. Group of sorority girls staggered out of some new cocktail lounge, swaying atop their heels—the exact name of the place doesn't matter, maybe Ofay's. That sound right to you, Uncle Joe? Ofay's?"

"Yeah, that sounds about right. Might as well have been anyhow. Matter of fact, maybe there was an apostrophe after that 'O'—like it was an Irish joint: Rick O'Fay's. Ha!" He chuckled without smiling. Max didn't understand but knew enough not to join them in laughing.

"Well, there was a homeless man resting on a bench at a DART bus stop hollering at these girls as they walked by. Maybe he said some lewd shit. Maybe he didn't. I don't know, but one of them also claimed he grabbed at her expensive-ass dress as she waltzed by. Now this cat had, according to other witnesses, been singing hymns and talking to himself long before his exposure to these fine, upstanding white girls. Oh, I should mention that he was African American, twenty-something, and about six feet tall. That description, it turns out, was enough to get my cousin killed. So, one of them had a boyfriend along with her, and he gets up in this dude's face and is cussin' and spittin' and just lookin' for an excuse to take a swing when a bus pulls up. The homeless man shoves him out of the way and hops on the bus, probably just trying to get away. Now this frat guy's piping mad that he didn't get to knock the teeth, whatever were left of them, out of that big black mouth. Well, by now the lady that got her Gucci dress grabbed on is over it and wanting keep drinking, so she's begging her boyfriend to let it go, and if he had obeyed his woman, my cousin would still be alive. Instead, he calls the police and gives them this description: black, twenty-something, about six feet tall. Doesn't even bother mentioning that the dude is homeless and probably schizophrenic. Naw, he wouldn't have said all that, because he didn't see it. I guess to him, all black folks wear torn rags and talk to they selves at the bus stop. You a smart guy, Maximillian, so I suppose you already know what happens next."

"I—I don't know." He did and he didn't. But, what did that matter? His words weren't the ones that needed to come next.

"Trey was a junior at Atena State. Came home for the weekend for this man here, his father's, birthday." Reggie kept his arm aimed at Uncle Joe as if he were afraid to drop it, while the latter muttered something and glowered at the street. His face was dark—a steely ashen hue that emitted something along the spectrum of anger and pride. "He took the A-train from Atena to downtown Dallas, where he transferred to a bus. Got off here right by the bar, which was hosting a barbecue for this old war hero's birthday, and as soon as he stepped foot off that bus, he heard shouting, white folks' voices, and saw bodies charging him. He pulls out his hand, which was clutching his phone, from the pocket of his True Religions, and the mother fuckers got spooked—thought it was a weapon—and one of them unloaded his clip, even while his partner yelled, 'Don't shoot!'"

"Jesus," was all Max could think to say. And then, "I'm so sorry, man." He knew he was supposed to say something to Uncle Joe too, but he couldn't look at the man. Words didn't seem big enough, and whose words would they be?

Reggie walked Max down the path they had come up—tracing dusky Carmichael back to glimmering Davis Street, which would eventually intersect with Granbury Drive. With the bars now closed, only the spectral incandescence of the streetlamps burned overhead—like suns orbited by the black penumbras of dancing June bugs—maintaining a flush of pale light that bathed the sparse streets.

"This as far as I go, Max. You can find your way from here. Gotta get back and help old Uncle Joe get home, drive his truck, I mean. He's a proud man, doesn't want to admit that he can't see so good in the dark anymore. Funny thing is, he was a 'lurp' in Vietnam: that's long-range reconnaissance patrol. Saw everything with crystal clarity back then, even with the enemy all around him. But now, surrounded by friends, now everything's fuzzy. That's just life, isn't it? That's the American way, huh Max?"

"Yeah, I guess so. Look, Reggie, before you go, I need to ask you about what you said earlier." The alcoholic effervescence that had lifted him earlier had now fallen heavy throughout his extremities, pulling the soles of his feet to the flat earth below. "You said you knew." Reggie, who had turned away, pirouetted with surprising ease. "You knew, um, why I did all that." Something that had been flickering within Reggie's eyes throughout the night was now fanned into a flame, unnerving Max.

"You haven't learned shit tonight, boy. You spent a decade trying to learn something, and you didn't learn shit then. Didn't learn shit tonight either."

"Fuck off, dude. You come across acting all wise and suave taking white guys on God damn night tours of the neighborhood. But there's no point, no conclusion. It just ends with a few wasted hours and an empty feeling. What am I supposed to do with that?"

The two stood with square shoulders only inches apart, regarding each other with drooping eyes that squinted back to life. Then, Reggie laughed. "Boy, you watch too many movies or something. I'm not your fucking negro spirit guide. I ain't Morgan Freeman. And what's this bowing up to me with your white indignation? Your body acting like a man, but inside you're a lost little boy." Max opened his mouth to say something, but Reggie raised his palm. "No, we ain't gonna fight like a couple kids. I respect that you're trying to be a man. You been trying for years, but you just can't quite reach it, can you? Taking a swing at me sure as hell isn't gonna get you there. Listen, Max, I can't interpret your fucking stories from the road for you because that shit never happened!"

"That's bullshit, Reggie. Complete bullshit. My best friend is dead, man! That's not real enough for you?"

"I believe your boy is dead. That I do believe. Shit, maybe most of those stories you told me tonight happened in one form or another. But they didn't happen the way you're remembering them. Look, you spent years trying to find yourself or whatever you wanna call it, but that's not what you actually did. You were just a kid drinking a lot and refusing to grow up. You were a bored white boy, and you had a guy who was also a bored white guy and you drove off into Neverland, before eventually, years later, crashing back into planet Earth and seeking some greater meaning from all of it. That's all well and good, but when black folks want to *find* themselves they usually end up *finding* themselves in places like Khe Sanh or lying face first in the blood-soaked pavement of south Dallas."

"Yeah, I suppose," began Max, his mind spinning and draining the anger from him. "I suppose there's some truth to that." He felt a cool breeze brush across his forehead, soothing him in a way, the first break from the summer night's oppressive heat. His words still weren't right, but he knew it was right that he was saying them. Then, as a sort of metamorphosis—a breathing to life of the fresh wind condensing around him—he felt sprinkles of rain from the black sky splashing against his white forehead. This grew. Soon, it was all around them, a deluge, unheard of for August in Texas. Both men stood, motionless, facing one another, and it was through watching Reggie's clothes soak and sag around him that Max became aware of his own dripping condition, which washed the sweaty filth from their tired bodies and cooled their feverish minds.

"Some truth? Hell, that's the whole truth, man."

"I'm beginning to see that that's true too. This is going to sound silly and—and well, it's really a small detail—but I was reading a lot of Hemingway back then. We would take *The Sun Also Rises* with us for nearly every road trip and would read some passages again and again." Atheists' bible, Max thought to himself, even though that wasn't quite right.

"Yeah, man and what ends up happening in the end?" With both men soaked, their clothes crumpled and clinging to them, there was no more swagger, no posturing. They just were.

"Oh, well they don't end up together, even though they could have." Funny, he thought, *could have* had always struck him as the cruelest phrase in the English language—what killed Sam. At that moment he realized how wrong he was. "There was nothing stopping them but themselves—and World War I."

"No, I'm not talking about the book. Matter of fact, I never read it. Max, your life is not a fuckin' story! I'm talking about the man: Ernest Hemingway. How did *he* end?"

"Since you're asking, I guess you already know

that he shot himself." He was about to say something else but stopped instead and sighed. "OK, OK, I see your point."

"This rain," said Reggie, "is a warning. There's another hurricane coming—Harvey—that's supposed to mess up Houston in a couple days."

"Yeah, I've been hearing about that. They've got those flashing marquees on all the interstates warning against traveling to the Gulf of Mexico. Guess it's going to be bad. Can't be as bad as Katrina though, right?"

"Nah. Nah, how could it be? That's a once in a lifetime kind of event."

Wordlessly, they began to step away from one another, each man plodding off in his own direction. Then, Reggie turned one last time toward his companion and said this: "Max, I'm sorry about your buddy, Sam. I mean—I get it. I know what he meant to you."

"Thank you for understanding, Reggie."

"Yeah, I could say the same to you."

Brett was leaning against the wall in the space that separated their two doors when Max stomped down the hallway in the wee hours of the morning. Her eyes were bloodshot, and her face looked as if the makeup had melted down it, like a candle left alone too long in an abandoned room. She pawed at her face, catlike, upon spotting Max. Limply dangling from her other hand was a lit joint that, forgotten, had burned into just a black smoky stub.

"Maxwell," she said, regarding him sideways. "I know you weren't out drinking all night, so that means you were up to something else. And that's cool, guy.

Who was she tonight? Caroline? God, anyone but
Caroline. No, come on, we're just friends, right? We
can talk about these things. Indulge me and—"

"Brett! Darling! I don't know that I've ever called
anyone 'darling' before—like some sort of Humphrey
Bogart character from the Fifties or something—"

"Oh shit you're hammered." Brett's face seemed to
unclench into something softer.

"No, no, not hammered. Well, OK, I dabbled a
little with this Reggie character I met tonight, but
mostly I'm just tired now." He leaned over and hugged
her confidentially, warmly.

"Max, you're not supposed to—I mean I thought
you don't do that. Wait, who's Reggie? That's a guy."

"Come inside, let's talk about it. I'll tell you all
about this dude if you can stay up until dawn and hear
it." He held his door open for her and led her inside,
upon which he snuffed out her joint by pressing it into
an ashtray. After securing her within his sheets, he
undressed and paused before tossing aside his jeans,
feeling the weight of his phone, cold, singular beneath
the thin sheath of fabric that had been warmed by his
active flesh and then bathed by the summer rain. Then,
he tossed the jeans, phone and all, into a crumpled heap
in the corner. With her last waking moment, Brett
propped her head onto Max's bare chest and muttered,
"OK, tell me about Reggie."

The following morning, after homemade waffles
stuffed with pecan halves and eggs scrambled together
with bright salsa into a punchy pink, and then Brett's
departure to shower at home, Max went to the gym. He
hadn't felt the pinch of a hangover in years, and his
body was in full revolt. After ibuprofen and coffee and

soda and all his old standby remedies, he thought the only sensible option left was to sweat out the poison that still circulated throughout his aching body. He set the treadmill timer to 50 minutes and began. The flesh surrounding him seared and shook, drooping down like a tablecloth baked by afternoon sun into a toasty crunchiness. Skin—feverish, taut was cooled by the strange chill of sweat. His steps, intentional, fell clumsily, heavily and with great difficulty, as if the strain of a lifetime accompanied each one. Soon, though, the enflamed tendons and seized musculature eased as if a draught of oil had begun percolating through the unseen circuitry of life. In his past he had coexisted easily enough with the toxins, following them into madness and exultation, but unaffected. Once, many years ago when he had forgotten about a date to meet Jessica at the Atena State Rec Center, he arrived anyway, late, after drinking a six-pack at home—and proceeded to run four miles around the indoor track. She couldn't keep up with him. And so it was. With margins wide as oceans, he had persisted, forever swimming from the shore and seeking Atlantis. He thought warmly now of Jessica. She may have been all wrong for him at the time (who wasn't?), but that was no excuse to have treated her so badly.

Then he thought differently about Caroline—not coldly but from a scholarly distance. He considered their mutual erosion of one another and how it wasn't all for naught. Or was it? No, surely not. Still, what impressed him the most was his newfound objectivity on the subject. But still . . . but still . . .

He checked his progress against the downward counting timer. Since he hadn't faced his old nemesis, the 50-minute 10K, in years and was only casually jogging these days, he had begun this run absent of expectations, especially hungover. So, he was surprised to see his pace had left him only slightly off target. The clock revealed 3:40 remaining with 5.7 miles completed. Only a half-mile remained. He remembered that the world record holder, a guy named Hicham El Guerrouj, ran an entire mile in just 3:43. Max smacked the up arrow a few times and shook his body, depleted, dehydrated into a new phase, shrugging off the burning in his chest and the stiffening in his joints. All he needed now was to run halfway to an impossible mile time. And he was going to make it too. The phone buzzed to life and Max ignored it for a moment or two until he noticed the name glowing across it.

"Hello, Max!"

"Hey!" He stopped the timer and stepped off the whirring treadmill. "I'm so happy to hear from you!"

"Yeah?"

"Yes. Guess what?"

"What . . . "

"We did it, Brett."

2005

Max lingered on the balcony awaiting his marching orders while Sam cased the upstairs bar. There was a green corrosive tint to the sky and frenetic charge to the floating crowd below. Girls walking down Bourbon were staider than in the past, wobbling along with knowing smiles and shirts that remained on. A bitter scent of blue-green algae blooms drifted over the city from Lake Pontchartrain. He checked his phone: a recent upgrade from a plain Nokia 3210 to Motorola Razr V3 with a colorful screen that popped to life when it was flipped open. No message yet from Sam. Running low on beer, he spun around toward the interior when a tall woman in heels bumped him, splashing her drink across his shirt.

"Oh, shit. I'm so sorry, dude. Now I'm *that* girl, you know, the drunken lush who just makes a mess of everything. Except I'm not that drunk." Maybe she only looked tall, as some women have a way of doing.

"It's OK, really. This happens to me at least three times a night on Bourbon Street, and most girls don't apologize." She was really quite striking, pleasantly smirking despite her folded arms. She wore a beige summer sweater that would have been appropriate on Cape Cod, perhaps, but was almost gallingly defiant in their southern setting in August.

"You sure it's OK? You're not just saying that to be a gentleman? I really didn't plan to be an obnoxious bitch tonight, though these days I just can't seem to help it." Her smirk morphed into something else.

"Yeah, you're good. In fact, to prove how OK I am, let me get you a replacement drink since you spilled most of that one. I was on my way to the bar anyway."

"Not necessary. I drink for free here, so how 'bout I be the one to get us drinks. I used to work here. Few years back. Just for a hot minute really, but I've been hanging out ever since. Shit, am I a lush? Let me get you some wahtah too to clean yo' shirt. B-R-B, sweets." There was something utterly disarming about that Creole accent, the way it just sort of slurred out of women's mouths at the tired ends of phrases. It reminded him of New Jersey gangsters in movies but was safely locked within the familiarity of a southern drawl. He wondered if they'd crossed paths during the long sequence of trips. Quite likely.

He watched as she flitted away. There was something out of season about her, a certain gait or maybe smile that seemed like it belonged to someone else. Nothing about her matched, yet she carried herself as if she were an actress coached to walk with poise.

Pouring out beneath her sweater was a flowy black hem that was nearly translucent. It was as if she'd asked a boyfriend for whatever sweater he happened to be wearing and draped herself in it, except this was no man's outerwear.

His phone buzzed, and of course it was Sam. "Found her. Come to the downstairs bar. Now!" Jesus, Max thought. He needs backup—the presence of another body to vouch for his sanity. A lone man seeking a woman is a stalker, but the presence of a single other person upgrades them to a party. Meanwhile, Max had already confirmed that there was no Electra. Oh, the idea of her may have been real enough to Sam, but she was merely a voodoo whisper in the New Orleans night, a myth. Perhaps there had once been an exotic girl who had flooded Sam's unprimed synapses with the sheer rawness of her femininity. He had made up first a name and then this fiction must have blossomed into full-fledged romance as the progenitor became more and more infatuated with his own conception of what he'd lost in his youth—crippled by spiritual guilt and paralyzed by the promise of hellfire. But who awaited him downstairs? Max didn't want to know. What parent would choose to be present for the moment her child's faith in the Easter Bunny is shattered?

"So what's your name anyway?" The girl had returned with two rum and Cokes. He recognized the sweet scent of molasses before even taking a sip. "You look familiar. Ever come in here a few years back when I would have been working the bar?"

"It's probable, actually. I'm Max. My buddy and I have been coming here for years."

"Oh, so maybe we've met. I'm Callie. Or, not *met* exactly, but maybe you yelled out a drink order once while staring at my tits and I gave you a bitchy look and overcharged you."

"That sounds about right." He laughed, while she just smiled and seemed to search his face. "Yeah, no, but seriously that name does ring a bell. I think maybe—maybe you were working the bar back when we first started coming here? Back in 2002?"

"Yeah, yes! In the wintertime, right? I worked here from the previous summer and kind of tapered it off— eventually quit—during the next fall after I started back at school at Southeastern Louisiana. So you and this friend, if he's real—'cause you know I don't see anyone standing there with you—you must be locals, right?"

"Um, no we actually live in Texas. This is embarrassing but—we've been here probably a dozen times since 2002."

"Shit, dude. Why, you got a girl here or something?"

"No, but he thinks he does."

"What?" It wasn't a question. She folded her arms, dangling her cup past her elbow with only her index finger and thumb. She flipped her head back, regarding him as if through bifocals, bouncing her blond hair out of her neatly straightened bob. Maybe it wasn't a bob. It was some variation of Jennifer Aniston's trademark past-the-chin layers. "So's she imaginary or something?"

"She's supposed to be a bartender here, and he claims he's wooing her right now at the downstairs bar. He's asking me to come down and meet her, so I guess he's cornered someone, but the girl he's seeking is a myth."

"You two aren't like other guys on Bourbon, are you?" Her face teetered between limp amusement and cautious rigidity, and he detected the subtlest tinge of redness spread across her cheeks that could have come from either the alcohol or the heat. Or maybe it just came from her, Max thought, as he tried to understand why he found her so utterly adorable. Her questions were never quite questions yet not entirely rhetorical either. It was as if she were psychically willing her thoughts into his head while outwardly feigning conversation just to keep up appearances. She would have seemed disinterested if her face hadn't glowed with such a mixture of sincerity and—something else. "It's cool. You don't want to be like all the shithead dudes out here. Trust me. And, I hope I don't come across as just another one of these silly drunken hoes that are everywhere, screaming and grinding on the dance floor with any old frat boy who pushes up against them. And I love dancing, nothing wrong with that, but do they have to be so mindless about it? I shit you not, once when I was working the bar, I saw a girl grinding so hard into a guy that he had to rush off to the bathroom to clean himself up." Max had been nodding along, just enjoying her voice (which had a timbre that registered just a few notes above the buzz of the crowd), but this last tidbit seemed meaningful through her willingness to share it with him. "I think a lot of these girls, the white ones anyway, come from old money all over the South. It's funny how family money offers women the golden ticket to be absolutely useless. I like to have fun. Who doesn't? But, I'm about to start my second year in grad school, in social work, and I already have serious student loans, y'know?"

"Oh, that's great—that you're in grad school, not the student loans part. Are you still at Southeastern Louisiana University?"

"Wow, see how you're different from other guys on Bourbon Street? You were actually listening to me. And yes, I graduated with a Bachelors in Social Work a year ago and then started a graduate program to get my Masters and LCSW certification." His phone had buzzed several more times, nestled deep within his jeans' pocket, but he didn't dare interrupt her at this point.

"So, when you're licensed, then you can counsel patients, right? Kind of like a therapist?"

"Yes, exactly. I really want to counsel children who have been abused. Y'know—sexually, especially those who have been victimized by a family member, like their stepdad or something, and they don't have an advocate or support system since the parents control their lives—purse strings and all. I know that sounds weird, but it's something that I—well I feel strongly about—." She was searching his face and seemed to be inviting him with her eyes to interrupt her. "—I guess because I've seen how much those wounds can linger or even grow deeper into adulthood." He smiled at her without a touch of flippancy. It was perhaps the purest expression he had made by that point of his life, and it originated deep within some unilluminated chasm within him. He had never felt so afraid. "What? Why am I telling you all this?" She wrinkled her eyes into something that very much resembled a smile, and Max thought he may have noticed a sparkle that she quickly blinked away. "Your friend. Let's go see what poor girl he thinks he's in love with. Hmm, all the bartenders working downstairs are really new, so it couldn't be them. Well, except for one: Sue."

"Sue? That can't be her." They squeezed their way down the stairs in no particular hurry.

"Yeah, but she spells her name S-i-o-u-x, like the Indian tribe."

"Wow, that's quite a name, but his girl's name is even weirder: Electra."

"Max!" Callie froze a few steps from the landing and hooked a bony hand around his shoulder to flip him back around toward her.

"Yeah, I know, sounds made up, right?"

"Sweetie, no, you've got it backwards. 'Sioux' is the made-up name." She cocked her head and sort of hugged herself with her tightly folded arms, shimmying gently from side to side, awaiting the burst of recognition that would in a nanosecond flood his face.

"Ah! Electra is real?! And she's here?"

"Yeah, she's here sometimes. Sometimes she's not. I know her, I suppose, in a way. Is she the one? She's his grand obsession? You're sure about that?" She sort of laughed in a shivery way and clapped her hands together.

"Sam doesn't like to call it 'obsession' but yeah, 'Electra' is definitely the name."

"Huh." She stared past him into a void of imagined years, attempting to solve some social equation in her mind. Max was about to interrupt her trance and yank her back to earth, infinitely curious as he was about her ominous utterance. She had, in the brief moments they had been talking, not once been tongue tied. Either she spoke with a confident, steady volley of syllables or she chose not to and simply stared at him, permitting and expecting his contribution. Speech seemed to be a birthright for her, and he could see beyond the roughened edges of the Creole drawl into an upbringing replete with parochial schools, tutors, esteemed teachers, and blue ribbons. He wondered how she didn't end up at Tulane or Vanderbilt or one of the other southern debutante private universities. Then she spoke: "I just wonder if your friend is enough for her."

Before Max could process this statement, another thought surfaced, unnerving him. "Wait, I've asked other girls here about Electra on many occasions, and none of them ever gave the slightest recognition. I've seen Sam do it too, and it never gets us anywhere."

"There's so much turnover at this place that most of the girls don't really know each other. Most only know their coworkers by the names on their shirts. Mine was 'Saffron.' I was a bartender, and occasionally we worked at the same station together a few years back, so I know her name. None of the shot girls would, I don't think. And, if he had gone around asking about 'Sioux' they would have assumed he was another stalker and pretended they didn't know anything. He probably figured that out pretty quickly. Plus, she's gone through a few nametags over the years. Sometimes we trade or lose ours or simply get bored with it and need a new name. There's a good chance she wasn't even 'Sioux' when he first met her."

As it turned out, she wasn't "Sioux" when Max met her either. He and Callie found Sam pinned up against the bar with his torso twisted toward the familiar face of a bartender Max had seen before but never noticed. Her nametag read "Taposa." She was short and petite but not in the stately, spindly way that Callie floated about. What appeared at first to be bruises were, upon closer inspection, cerulean mockingbird tattoos that had dulled into midnight blue puffs across her bare shoulders that resembled plumes of toxic smoke from burning oil. The blackness of her hair, which she'd yanked back into a mid-length ponytail, combined with her olive complexion to project a swarthy exterior that must have swallowed up invitations to a diverse range of social situations since she seemed to match all settings. When the fluorescent gold glow of the beer cooler behind her illuminated her features as she knelt down for a pair of Abitas, her lips looked thin and unassuming, like a child's, and her round cherub face revealed the mild droop of a double chin. Within the shadow of the bar station, she sort of pleasantly slid from one customer to the next, returning men's laughs and shouts with shrugs and an enticing upturn of her mouth that unmistakably said, "Go ahead."

Sam saw them and swiveled around, nearly knocking the glass out of the hand of a thin Black man who rolled his eyes. He reached past the guy, unaware, and slapped Max's hand, as if they were frat dudes meeting at the house for a themed party, which in a sense they were, he thought. Sam never gave high-fives.

The bartender (who was calling herself Taposa and had previously been Sioux and probably half a dozen other appropriated names, but was really maybe Electra) noticed Max for the first time. Or rather, she recognized Callie and noticed that someone was with her. The two made a hand gesture between them and then she filled two glasses with a clear liquor and soda water and reached over both the black man and Sam to hand them to the other woman.

"Thanks, sweetie," said Callie. She removed the pale straws from each before handing Max his glass and blowing Electra a kiss.

"You know this guy, doll?" She pointed down at Sam and laughed, revealing crooked teeth and the silver sheen of a midline tongue piercing.

"Naw, but I know his cute little friend here." She patted him on his chest with her palm.

"Oh, dude," she said to Sam, "you do have a friend." She laughed again and then shouted toward Max over the thumping Black Eyed Peas song vibrating through the mounted speakers and the shrieks of tourists to each other as well as the Russian shot girls. "I thought you were just his imaginary friend!" She coughed out another burst of laughter. A horde of guys had just shoved their way off the dance floor and were slapping their hands against the bar, demanding Electra's attention, and so she slid over to them. She was far enough away that Max couldn't understand what she was saying to the sweaty young guys, but he saw her smile and cock her head to the side like a puppy. As she took an order from one of them, she winked at another. Even when she wasn't laughing, which was rare, she kept her dark eyes locked onto them and bent her lips upward into what must have looked to them like a toothless smile. She finished pouring rows of shots in front of them and taking their wads of cash and then walked back over. "Babe, you'll love this," she said to Callie. "I just charged them all

Patrón prices for well tequila. You know how it is—
gotta protect my ass in case they don't tip. You never
know with these jokers."

"And did they tip you?" asked Sam. Then he added
(to Max, under his breath), "in addition to your hot girl
premium surcharge."

"Oh yeah, guys always do."

Callie, meanwhile, had been pawing at Max for a
while with increasing fervor. Finally, she squeezed his
shoulders and pressed him downward, bringing him
almost to his knees. She had a test tube of yellow
liqueur half-submerged between her lips, and she tilted
his head back and poured the sweet liquid from her
mouth into his, as if she were a shot girl. She signaled
again to Electra with her hand, which produced another
clear cocktail. This one she gulped at a few times and
then held it to Max's lips. She was about to pour this
one into his mouth too until he wrested it from her hand
and sipped delicately—already feeling his head
swimming and his stomach churning, as his body
struggled to digest the sudden invasion of sugar and
alcohol within him. Impatiently, she took the glass from
him the way a parent plucks a dangerous object from a
toddler's hand and left it on the bar. Instead she took his
hand and yanked him out to the dancefloor, sliding her
body against him.

A little after midnight, Max and Callie wobbled
back over to the bar to say their goodbyes to the others.
She had invited him to her apartment in Metairie, which
sounded far to him but was (she assured him several
times) a short cab ride. He knew well enough from the
exit signs along I-10 when driving to New Orleans that
it was only a few miles from the French Quarter, but

somehow the process of leaving the neighborhood, jumping onto the interstate, and traveling to an entirely separate town—one doubtless filled with families in middle-class houses and mortgages and savings accounts and all those other anchors that moored one helplessly to their responsibilities—felt like a meaningful departure. He couldn't picture Callie here slurping shots and kissing him wildly on the dance floor, only to drift back into a phase of sensible domestication in a suburb. It was a problem of time. The French Quarter existed in the present, while everywhere else swirled hopelessly into the future. As they were about to leave, Sam grabbed at Max's shoulder.

"So, you see it, right? I'm not delusional or whatever you and Benson think of me. I wasn't sure at first—I mean she was talking to me a lot. A lot. Sure, yeah, I was buying drinks, but then, then she started just pouring them for me." Electra was gone. Her shift had apparently ended, so she was off in some back room submitting cash and receipts. Without her "Taposa" nametag and skimpy royal blue uniform stretched around her breasts, Max wondered who would emerge from the black hallway past the doorless restrooms in the back of the club. "It wasn't about money because I wasn't giving her any. That means something, right? It has to!" Sam was wide-eyed, mindlessly shifting his weight from one foot to the other in a way that wasn't quite nerves but rather a surge of dopamine as if he'd just taken a hit of something.

"I don't know, man. She was flirting her way to the bank all night." Callie had hooked her arm around his and was tugging at him impatiently. "But—sure, it might mean something. Yeah, it had to. She spent her entire shift talking to you." He honestly couldn't tell if he meant it, but Callie's importunities helped him say it, for one reason or another.

"Yes, YES! That's the point; I stopped spending money and she kept pouring. She didn't do that for anyone else. Yes, the rest of it was fake, just bullshit for tourists; I'm not naïve. But, not with me!"

"Dude, just don't go all weird on her, OK? Don't be a creeper!" Callie was already walking away and tugging Max's arm as if it were a dog's leash. "Don't be an obsessive stalker, sweetie!"

"Jesus, NO!" Sam yelled back. "Where are you two even going? She's coming back in a few minutes. We could all go somewhere together—"

"Sammy, Samantha, whatever the fuck your name is. Listen to me. She maybe likes you a little. You maybe like her a lot. The thing with Electra is she likes everyone and everyone likes her when she's—like this."

"What does that mean? What does that even fucking mean?" Sam was almost comically animated. He might have seemed angry to someone who didn't know him and his bursts of childish enthusiasm, the way he tossed swear words out there like they were a part of a carnival game.

"Guy, do I have to spell it out for you? Did you see her at the start of tonight's shift all sort of cold and lifeless and bitchy. Then, magically, after she took her first break and locked herself in a bathroom stall for a few minutes, she came back bursting at the seams and chipper and full of energy and all flirty and shit."

"Oh. I see." Sam seemed to search within himself

for a moment. "OK, whatever, so she gets a little high to put up with the ass hole guys on Bourbon Street. I'm sure she's not the only one at BBC doing that stuff."

"Samuel, she's coked out of her fucking mind most nights. When she's not, you don't want to be around her—the real her. Goodnight and good luck—maybe she'll actually come back and talk to you instead of just slipping out the back door and off into the night. Because, you know, she left with a Hollywood actor the other night, and he might still be in town."

Callie yanked Max away from the bar, away from Sam's volley of questions, away from the sloppy collision of sweaty bodies on the dance floor. She led them to a black Lincoln Town Car, a jitney evidently, and gave the driver an address. His quote sounded about right to Max, but Callie cursed at the driver, a middle-aged blond man with a patchy goatee and red eyes. His sparse tufts of pale hair were mostly bunched up above each ear like a pair of horns. Callie motioned for Max to follow her across the street to a gray minivan taxi that looked more official. The jitney driver shouted something at them with a gravelly bayou drawl and flicked a lit cigarette out the window, which bounced on the pavement before wedging into a crevice in the sidewalk where it just throbbed with its reddish glow, spewing streams of white smoke into the black night.

The cab pulled up to a modest, clapboard duplex on a green street lined with southern magnolias. Callie paid the taxi driver, offering an ample tip that more than covered what the first driver would have charged. She was sensitive to payments, Max observed, recalling her prideful insistence on only taking drinks served *gratis*, yet it wasn't exactly about the money itself. Maybe that was just the point—that it was about her pride, her measure of the value others saw in her.

One could not have predicted the chaos of the interior based on the banality of her home's exterior. She had painted each room a different earth tone, but because the space was so small, the hues all sort of stacked upon one another like a depressed rainbow. The kitchenette nook was ochre and opened into a living room with tawny walls. An open door from there revealed a bathroom that was a sort of burnt umber, and on the other side of that was another opening that led to a dull taupe bedroom. There was only room for a love seat in the living room and a pair of end tables that had been merged to approximate a coffee table. There were ashen-hued throw blankets draped atop the love seat, and dirty dishes in front of it on the little squat tables. On the scratched, sienna-colored hardwood floor was a conspicuously pink rug with a zigzag pattern stitched across it that resembled an EKG. On the living room walls were dozens of pictures in mismatched frames— some were decorative, hand-carved blocks of wood while others were simple bands of black plastic. Callie, herself, was centered in most of them, smiling with arms wrapped around friends (perhaps even some ex-lovers), chronicling her teenage years up to the present. On the kitchen counter was a hand of rotting bananas and a half-dozen wine bottles. Stacked beyond what the sink basin could accommodate were precariously stacked dishes.

"Ah, you're a wine connoisseur, I see," said Max. Callie was already lifting an opened bottle from the refrigerator.

"No, I'm a chardonnay connoisseur. Look for yourself. That's all I buy, but really I don't know much about wine. I know I like chardonnay, and since I'm picky, I only buy the one type. Every now and again I think I'm getting bored with it and so I try something new—something sweeter like sauvignon blanc—but I always end up going back to chardonnay. Can't stop myself. I'm obsessed!" It was true. They were all chardonnay and wrapped in those simple pastel labels with faux exotic names that one sees at any gas station in America. "Here." She filled two oversized glasses to the lip.

Max was again examining her framed photographs when Callie, who had tossed off her flats, approached him, carefully landing each step—her glass already half empty. No wonder she didn't wear heels, he thought. Even barefoot, she was at least an inch taller than he was. "Whatcha lookin' at?" She was consciously modulating her voice, alerted by some self-regulatory system that she was liable to slide into shrill drunken shouts at any time, and in fact, she had already breached that boundary a few times throughout the evening.

"All your lovely pictures. These all friends of yours with you? Or family?"

"No. Just friends." She was swaying gently and fingering at the buttons on his shirt. She gulped the latter half of her chardonnay and then glanced at his virgin glass. "Drink up, sweetie. Or, do you not like it? I think I have some beer in the refrigerator too, if you want something else."

"No, this is perfect. You're a model hostess." He took a long drink, after which she seized his glass and took a sip. "Let me help you out with that." Her free hand wandered down to his belt and began fumbling at the buckle. "Wait, who's the giant silver fox in this little polaroid. Jesus, he must be six foot six."

"The fuck?" She staggered back, locking her gray eyes onto the photograph with genuine astonishment. "I told her not to. I told that bitch to get that shit out of my home! I told her. I TOLD her!" She dropped his glass to the floor, splashing jagged fragments like transparent shrapnel over their feet.

"Oh, hey, don't move," said Max. "You're barefoot. Let me pick up all the pieces for you." She may or may not have heard him, but either way she was stomping away, hyperventilating and heaving deep choking sobs from her chest. This onslaught was so precipitous, so sudden that he felt nakedly unprepared. Through all his history with women, when they had cried to him, it had always been about him. But this was new—and terrifying. There was a different timbre to her cries that called to something primal buried deeper within her than the simple stinging pain of a faltering relationship. At that moment Max felt something he'd not yet experienced with a woman: the helpless distance from her, the inability to reach her and prop her back up with his words or deeds.

Callie crumpled to the ground in the bathroom, indistinguishable from the wrinkled laundry around her except for a trickle of blood from her foot. She was shaking and clutching herself in a lonely hug, still crying loudly the way that children do with more noise than tears. Max rummaged around in the kitchen until he found a broom and dustpan and a roll of paper towels. After absent-mindedly cleaning the mess (being largely unable to look away from the toppled body in the bathroom), he nervously slinked toward her and crouched down.

"I'm sorry. I'm so sorry. You don't have to be here." She had stopped sobbing but was nearly hyperventilating, her gray eyes dilated into pools of tar encircled by a sliver of shiny steel. "I'm not your problem. Just go. I'm sorry you saw this." The burnt umber paint on the walls made one feel buried within a mound of fecund soil. Callie's golden hair, in defiant contrast to the drab bathroom, danced along the stony, rectilinear tiles as she wretched about.

"No, I want to be here." He didn't wonder why he said it. "Just take slow, deep breaths, OK? Try to concentrate on your breathing," he said while stroking her hair in long, steady caresses of his fingertips. "I think you're having a panic attack. But, you're going to be OK." He had propped up her head onto his lap and was hugging her as best he could with his free hand, as he moved the other deliberately through her hair like a conductor during an adagio movement. "Do you want to talk to me about it?"

"The picture. I didn't put it there. Didn't want to see that face ever again." She was still panting, which accounted for the absence of syntax, but her torso was beginning to slow its contractions, and Max could sense a cool stillness begin to wash over her. "It's my dad. I spent my entire childhood, literally until I was a teenager, hiding from him and those big, gross hands that would—do things to me. About a year ago, after my mom's funeral, my aunt, which is my dad's sister, shows up with that picture and says she thinks it would be nice for me to have a photograph of my parents from when they were still together. Touching, right? No, it was a total bitch move on her part. She did it just to rub in my face that she'd never believed me about—what he did to me. Thought my mom put me up to it to screw him in the divorce. The truth is that she divorced him *because* of what he did to me."

"Oh God, Callie, I'm so sorry to hear all of this," Max said. He tasted the uselessness of his words even while speaking them. Still, he felt he needed to say or do something besides stroking her hair. Maybe that's not right at all, he thought. Maybe you just listen in these situations.

"Then, of course, even after my ass hole dad gets diagnosed with cirrhosis of the liver, he *still* outlives my poor mom, who died in a car wreck. Drunk driver."

"Jesus, Callie." He stopped himself from saying more. Instead, he asked her permission to search the bathroom cabinets for bandages and then, upon scrounging up some Disney Princess ones, sealed up her bleeding heel.

"Yeah, sorry, it's a lot to unload on you. I didn't mean to bring any of this up."

"It's OK. Tell me anything you want."

"Anyway, I had some choice words for my aunt that day and haven't spoken to her since. I didn't want to ever see her face or my dad's again. But yeah, it seems that the bitch secretly put it on my wall, and somehow I guess I mentally blocked it out until you noticed it."

"Oh, I didn't mean—I'm sorry about that." He felt a pang of guilt surge through his chest. So this *was*, at least indirectly, his fault?

"No, sweetie, no!" She twisted around on his lap

until she faced him and brushed her fingers across his cheek. "I was bound to see it at some point, and it would have been so much worse if I had been alone when it happened." She leaned upward and kissed him. "I'm embarrassed, sure, but I'm so, so grateful that you were here with me—whoever you are!" She laughed and began scraping herself off the floor.

"Let's get you to bed," said Max. He balanced her as she limped into the bedroom. The taupe walls surrounding them, which had looked dreary from his earlier vantage point, now seemed serenely meaningful, like an Easter egg awaiting a pastel bath. They both flopped onto the bed without undressing and held each other wordlessly, listening to one another's breathing and feeling the gentle rise and fall of their breasts until they locked into a solemn synchronization. With their bodies pressed against each other, arms intertwined, and warm cheeks blended together, they lay there inert—not even kissing but somehow sharing a sensual closeness that Max had never before experienced and in fact didn't know existed. Just as they both felt the threads of consciousness begin loosening around them, Max heard a soft voice say, "Please don't leave me like everyone else."

"I won't," he whispered back. He didn't wonder why he said it.

The next morning, Sam sat hunched at the foot of the bed in their room at the Ramada on Gravier, which sat just outside of the green glow of the Tulane Medical Center. He didn't seem to be watching the local news on the television or noticing the sallow face of the weatherman who was urging greater New Orleans residents to keep an eye on an event in the Atlantic where a depression had merged with a tropical wave. The cyclone itself was ineffectual but carried the latent capacity to become a hurricane within the next couple days.

"If it does, indeed, produce a hurricane," said the gray-haired man, "Then it could make landfall around the Florida Keys." The man looked very old and tired as he said this. He wasn't the weekend meteorologist. The station had recalled their star weekday weatherman and plugged him into a special segment that was interrupting some Sunday morning political roundtable show. Someone at the station was taking this seriously. "Or—" continued the man with a perceptible pause, "it could strike the Gulf Coast of Alabama, Mississippi, or even here in southeastern Louisiana. And, considering the volatility of the 2005 Atlantic hurricane season thus far this year, I would strongly suggest that our viewers prepare for the worst. I recognize that most New Orleanians have lived through hurricanes before and have become accustomed to hunkering down and riding them out, but please heed this warning. We are seeing an increased intensity of major weather events, and you may need to evacuate sooner rather than later if this thing materializes in the way we fear it could."

An angular bolt of morning sunlight leaked into the dark room through a narrow opening between the drapes that loosely hung like lips past the faux French casement window. The yellow sunlight blended with the red glow of the television to illuminate one side of Sam's cheek in an eerie orange. He didn't turn around when Max entered the room, instead dropping his face into his hands as if his neck could no longer bear the weight of his skull.

"I am not a man," said Sam, speaking into his palms. "I—I seriously don't know how I got this far in life, but I don't deserve it. Any of it. It's been all wrong, and now, you should just put me down."

"So," began Max, "I'm going to assume Electra wasn't interested. Just another customer then, right?"

"No, Jesus, *no*! That would have been so much better." He turned toward Sam, revealing bloodshot eyes that looked they were about to pop out. His hair was still gelled carefully into a part, and he was wearing the same gray polo from the night before, adorned now with a coral stain across the midsection that matched the fruity color of one of the shooters the girls served at BBC.

"Well, I also have quite the tale of what turned out to be—somehow, someway—a sexless night," said Max. It hadn't come out right. There was, he noticed, a lingering sourness in his mouth, and he suddenly fantasized about dunking his head in Lake Pontchartrain. "But yeah, more on that after this break," he joked, imitating the TV weatherman, who had just shone black satellite images of an Atlantic depression before passing off to a commercial. "So, she *was* interested, then, but something went awry?"

"She—" Sam mumbled something Max couldn't understand. He was still facing away, ostensibly toward the window but not exactly seeing through it. Instead he was just staring off into some interminable point of the future from within the insular space of the room. "We have to go back to BBC." He stood and faced Max for the first time. Sam's eyes were dilated, and his body, which vibrated with a frenetic energy, revealed bluish veins that framed his biceps and forearms. In Max's mind he was adamant, robustly refusing, even while he felt his body follow Sam out the door without demur.

Like wound-up zombies they staggered down the stinking pavement, which already glistened from droplets of sweat under the morning August light. They were almost to BBC when a woman stepped out of a voodoo shop on Bourbon Street and blocked their path. Draped over her black dress was a green gossamer shawl that sort of floated over her shoulders. Her dark curls leaked out of a velvet purple headwrap, and dangling from her ears were golden hooks that terminated within a hinged black enamel cover. Atop her breast was a small golden locket.

"It's too early in the day fo' you boys to be hurryin' so much. Slow down now, slow down and come inside." Sam gestured wordlessly, sidestepping her, but stopped when he saw Max lingering behind.

"Um, no thanks," Sam said, staring away from her and down the street. "Sorry, we gotta go. Come on, Max, time's of the essence."

"By the looks of things, ya both could use a little gris-gris bag in yo' left pocket. Keeps the evil spirits at bay and gets the good juju vibratin' within ya. Come inside and take a look; we got a whole mess of different colors. Tell me now, what sort of magic do you boys need?" She had fixed her eyes on Max. "What about you? Max, is it? Tell me what you want, Max."

"No. He doesn't need anything, sorry. Max, we have to be—"

"Oof, you always let him talk fo' you?"

"Oh, he's just—he's trying to catch a girl. What's a gris-gris?" Sam rolled his eyes and began to walk away.

"Hey, boy!" She called over her shoulder at Sam.

"Ya know there's no magic strong enough to tame a wild woman, ha ha! Ya hear me?" Then to Max: "As for you, I think I can help. You see, a gris-gris is a potent little bag of charms that helps you focus on your goals. But you gotta keep an open mind, which I trust is no problem fo' you—just not *too* open of a mind, ya know? There's a storm comin' this way. Ya gotta get right with the universe before it blows or else ya never know who or what will wash up on yo' shore. Now, you wanna step inside?"

"I would like to, but I really have to go after him." But he paused, gazing at her silently.

"Oh, I know you do. That's OK, you'll be back. Go on and catch up with him before he gets himself mixed up with some trouble he can't get out of."

"If you don't mind my asking, what's in the locket?"

She smiled at him. "All of New Orleans, baby. I got the whole damned city right here by my heart."

It was only midmorning, but the cover band had already set up for the day and were just tuning the guitars and testing the audio monitor before the day drinkers began circulating the Quarter in any sizable number. Sam ordered a schooner of beer at the downstairs bar as an opening to question the black bartender whom neither of them had ever seen before. The daytime staff, they remarked to one another, was like a photographic negative of the night crew, who were all white and reaping the monetary rewards of the prime shift. Max wondered if a business could be sued for segregation by time. Sam passed the beer off to Max, who dutifully sipped it. He had felt achy and sweaty—his casual ease displaced by the daytime luminosity of the southern sky, under which worker bee families could be seen shuffling about their productive lives—but after a few gulps of the cold yellow beer he was whole again, immersed once more in the ritual of the barroom world, the forever night.

"Hi, do you know a girl who works here named Electra?" Sam and the bartender regarded each other for a moment. "Or Sioux or Taposa or whatever other name she might have told you."

"Yeah. What about her?" She folded her bare arms and tilted up her pretty face that was rounded like a porcelain doll's.

"Do you know if she's coming in today? Is she working today, I mean."

"I would have to check the schedule," she said without moving an inch. It was at that moment that Max noticed her nametag of the day: Saffron.

"Oh—I see." Sam placed a twenty-dollar bill on the bar.

"And, dude—" she began, while scooping up the money and sliding it beneath the tight fabric of her uniform around her breasts. "Even if I did go check out the schedule, who says I should pass that information along to you? You're no one, just another customer."

"Right, got it." Sam placed two more twenties on the bar before her. "Look, I'm not asking for her God damn address. I just need to know if she's coming in today."

"All right, man, here's the deal. She's crossed off the schedule for the rest of the month. Shit, we might be shutting down for a bit. You do know there's a hurricane coming, right? A lot of the girls are leaving town, going to stay inland with friends or family or whatever away from New Orleans. Most of us are leaving later this week and heading to places like Baton Rouge or Houston, but I heard that Electra left with that actor that's been coming in here to see her—err, he's not really an actor but from a reality show that was filming an episode in the Quarter. Can't remember his name, but yeah, she's supposed to be riding out the hurricane with him in Hollywood or something like that."

Sam didn't say anything. He just stared at her, his face turning pale.

"Well, it's been a pleasure doing business with you, sir. Got any more questions? Ha!" Her lips, smiling for the first time, were gallingly crimson, and her hair fell perfectly about her head like the branches of a weeping willow. She was reveling in this.

Sam muttered something and walked away. Max saw him climbing the stairs, perhaps to check out her information for himself. He didn't follow, instead finishing the beer and then paying for another on his own.

* * *

On the drive back to Texas, Sam alternated between wild bursts of ideas and silence. One moment he would be dissecting the timeframe of the coming storm and logistically working through every possible scenario for Electra's return to New Orleans. "Remember Hurricane Ivan?" he asked at one point. "It just came and went and—and everything was still possible." Then he wouldn't say a word for long stretches of time, sometimes even switching off the radio. Max had driven them away from New Orleans, past Baton Rouge, and up into Evangeline Parish, when they switched. Sam, driving for the first time, kept lifting his eyes from the highway, staring off somewhere in the vast blue sky. His face was sallow. Any time Max attempted to joke with him or mock the lyrics on the radio, Sam only grunted, if that, in response. Speech seemed to have washed away from him, floating downriver back to the steaming city and out into the hopeful, oceanic pool of the past. Max, giving up on him, began daydreaming about Callie, continuing in his mind conversations that had begun early that morning before they'd been snuffed out by the blanketing daylight and all its sobering implications—checkout times, work schedules, credit card payments, and all the other stumbling blocks toward the future. Max had met women on many drunken nights while stumbling around either the Atena town square or the French Quarter, but he'd never before had a person spill herself to him with such howling abandon. Even in the sober moments of the early dawn, she offered confessional recitations of her innermost pleasures and pain. Delving into her graduate program, she beamed, sharing quirky anecdotes of her gerontology course, though it wasn't her specialization. She also cited conversations with therapists regarding excruciating details of her father's abuse. Her even-tongued enunciation and nearly professional intonation suggested something other than catharsis, but rather that he had a right to know.

Suddenly, Sam let go of the wheel.

"What—what the hell?" yelled Max, suddenly recognizing the car veering off from the right lane toward the shoulder. He snapped upward, wide-eyed, as he felt the car shaking beneath him and the kazoo-sounding buzz of the rumble strips. They were soon gliding away from the paved shoulder toward the emerald marshes of the surrounding landscape. Their speed hadn't appreciably slowed, which Max quickly recognized as proof that Sam wasn't braking—or intending to change his mind, even as they headed for a cluster of enormous bald cypress trees.

"Ugh," said Sam, although it might have been something else. Max reached for the steering wheel. And right before fully merging with the green landscape and smacking into a wall of centuries-old tree trunks, he corrected their course and set them wobbling violently back onto the highway. Their sudden thrust back into the right lane caused another driver to screech the brakes and slip into a full 360-degree spin that finally came to rest on the shoulder. Sam, perhaps shaken from the cruel cellars of his mind and back into the present, gripped the wheel once again and steadied their movement as if nothing had happened.

"What the hell!" Max was panting, ready to pounce again, if the need arose. "What was that? Did you see what you did to that other car? And—and not to mention that we almost died!"

"Oh," began Sam with an eerie serenity. "Sorry, I guess you want to live."

* * *

On a lonely night in Atena a few days later, Max was roused by a mysterious knock. Standing on his porch was a ghostly figure who couldn't have been alive except for the vibrancy of the rain dripping down matted tufts of blond hair and ceremoniously dancing down her body in the moonlight.

"Am I dreaming?" Max drank from the aura of this visitor. Distrustful of his own eyes, he closed them for a moment, but still he knew—he could feel her presence before him.

"It's been a long journey among the slow drip of the hurricane refugees on the highway. We ran out of gas twice and then the engine overheated. Three days later, I'm here."

"Jesus, three days?" His eyes searched the night sky, guiltily knowing that somewhere past his realm of knowing, legions of underfed people (at least he imagined them that way) were struggling through the night—Americans who wanted to live.

"It's only time. You get more of it. Or you don't and you die. But right now I'm alive."

"I just can't believe you're here! What made you choose me?"

"I'm with you in Texas. That's all that matters." They stood for a moment, basking under the wan light of a crescent moon that had peeked out, briefly, from behind the gauzy veil of the Texas sky and its dark cotton clouds. "You gonna make me invite myself in?"

They sat across from one another at his cedarwood table that was too small for a kitchen built of aspirational proportions. The house was a cottage-like, one-bedroom rental in Atena near the interstate that led to Dallas. Max offered her a glass of chardonnay, but she refused and asked for green tea instead. Having already poured two glasses, he gulped one and brought the other to the table, while awaiting the kettle's whistle. They should have been eye-to-eye with one another, but Callie sat slumped in her chair.

"Are you really here?" He looked her over and understood that she was the same person but also wasn't. She seemed like a character inspired by Callie but bent in a new artistic direction by some unseen director. Her damp blond strands that clung to her chin framed her face with a silvery sheen in the lamplight, and her gray eyes had been galvanized such that they appeared now a steely navy blue.

"I'm with you in Texas. It was time to get moving, and so I did, and the winds blew me here—for better or worse."

"You're really here!"

"I came here because—I don't know why. Shit, we barely know each other! All I know is that I did, and I'm here with you in Texas. I had to leave New Orleans because of the hurricane, and something brought me here. From now on, I've gotta more forward. I can't anymore linger in the numb safety of the past, the comfortable sting of familiarity. That's a deadlier toxin than the risks of the future. It has to be a clear-eyed step forward, and to do so, I have to murder my old self. New city, new apartment, new job, new relationship, and even—new name. 'Callie' is a shortening of my fully formed, God-given name—it's an underdeveloped version of me."

Something planted ages ago was sprouting from the latent fields of his mind, a childhood memory of his grandparents in Ohio. *Exalted and hallowed be His great Name.*

"My mom called me Callie growing up. My dad didn't. Once I got old enough to make decisions for myself about things like that, I went with my mom's version. And well, my mom's been dead for years, and maybe it's time to bury 'Callie' along with her."

"And your dad? Will he be eager to learn that naming rights have tilted back in his favor?"

"Max." She squeezed both of his hands at once and held them outstretched between them as if they were about to pray. *Throughout the world which He has created according to His Will. May He establish His kingship, bring forth His redemption and hasten the coming of His Moshiach.* "Max, I'm going to say this once and then never speak of it again. I need to bury my dad more than anything else. My mom's dead, my dad's dead to me. I won't ever be speaking to him again or even speaking *of* him. He knows this, and he knows why. He knows how he hurt me when I was a little girl." *In your lifetime and in your days and in the lifetime of the entire House of Israel, speedily and soon, and say, Amen.* "This isn't about choosing a version of my name that he preferred. It's about no longer *not* using my name because of him, because he owned it. It's always been mine, and I'm taking it back. I thought I was me before, but I was still existing in response to someone else. From now on, I'm not Callie."

"And who are you?"

"I'm Caroline."

Amen.

They sipped their drinks, silently regarding each other for a few minutes. Each studying the minutia of movements and gestures of the other, trying to understand a lifetime through that primordial human language that transcends speech. With so much left to be said, they were immobilized by the weight of it all and landed upon something resembling silent respect for one another. Caroline was still damp and shivering, even though she'd materialized out of a warm August night and had her bony frame buried within a black hoodie. Across her breast, "NOLA" was written in previously gold lettering that had been worn down into a cracked yellow.

"Where do we go from here? Do we just—stay together? Do people do that?" asked Max, breaking the silence.

"I literally have nowhere to go," said Caroline. "Who knows when I'll be able to go home, and when I do, there might be nothing waiting for me in New Orleans. My friends are all scattered across Texas and Louisiana at the moment, probably sleeping on couches of cousins or college buddies. I caravanned to the Dallas area with a neighbor and a former roommate, and we're all supposed to meet up with our respective old friends to crash for however long this takes. But, when I got to the area, it suddenly dawned on me: I don't want to hunker down with friends from the past. I want to start fresh with someone new. That's the only way to launch yourself into the future—otherwise you just keep cycling back through the same events of the past and wondering what went wrong. It's funny, you know?" She wasn't exactly laughing. "You probably don't even remember scribbling out your number and address before you left that morning. I suspect you were just helping me feel a little less alone in order to remedy your own guilt about heading back to your hotel. Can't say as I blame you, what with my freak out the night before. But, Max, listen to me, I'm not your problem. I'll leave any time you want. In fact—maybe I shouldn't have come here at all." She rose and began collecting her phone and keys and other jangly odds and ends from her purse that she'd strewn about the bare kitchen table. "I think I had better just leave before we start making mistakes."

"Caroline, can I kiss you now?" And with that, she rushed toward him, pressing her lips against his with surprising ferocity and hooking both hands around the back of his neck such that he couldn't have pulled away—even if he had wanted to. Then she softened her grip, her lips gliding against his mouth and her fingertips lightly tickling the hairs on the back of his neck. This final moment before she released him was intimate through its delicacy—a moment filled with the sweet, ephemeral newness of love's inimitable flicker between two conspirators who have first unmasked themselves to one another.

"But this is crazy, Max." Her eyes, only inches from his, were dark pools, like swamps in the night filled with their ominous potentiality. "You really want to give it a shot? You do realize that we've only met *once* before." She held her index finger above her head, as if she were gesturing toward God.

"Twice before." He held up two fingers, and she kissed them.

"Oh, you're right! Well, that makes this the third time. That *has* to mean something!" There was a mournful elation to the arc of her lips. She was cauterizing some old wound, Max sensed, knowing there was a price to be paid for closure.

"So, do we just live happily ever after?" It was a joke, but Caroline cocked her head and narrowed her eyes, focusing on some part of him. He looked past her at the spare, beige walls and wondered what else, besides herself, she would tote from her car and into his (*their*) little house. Would she shrink herself down into a piece of the machinery of his life, or would her spirit fill up the yet undefined spaces?

"You shouldn't talk of happily evah aftuh to a survivor of childhood abuse." He hadn't noticed her Creole accent until just then.

"Oh, Caroline, I'm sorry, I wasn't—"

"It's OK. No biggie, sweets! But listen to me, Max, happily ever after is dangerous. It's bullshit because it's irrelevant. Life is just a collection of moments—some happy, some sad—and how they begin and end has nothing to do with anything. Those of us who've experienced childhood trauma know that the pain doesn't end when the abuse ends. But, we hope to bury the shitty moments under a mound of happy ones. If you were to dissect your life and reorder all the events, what would you find? Right now, I feel happy being here with you, and I think we should pursue that with all our hearts and keep trying to enjoy that happiness for as long as we are able. People make too much of time, which is lunacy since we can't ever know how much of it we even have."

"Well," he smiled. "Then perhaps we're perfect for one another because people are always accusing me of being late."

"Nah, the rest of the world's just early!" She threw her arms around him and laughed, as Max felt the dampness of her cheek against his.

"Caroline, I don't know why, but I think we will be OK."

"I think I like that about you." She pulled back

from their embrace to look him in the eye. "I don't know what we will be, but I'm happy with you right now. Doesn't that mean something?"

About the Author

M.R. Koch's short fiction, poetry, and scholarly essays have been published across both domestic and
international journals and literary magazines. He holds an MA in English from the University of North Texas
and a PhD in American literature from Texas Christian University. Currently, he serves as a Professor of
English at a Dallas-area college, where he teaches creative writing, composition, and American literature.

More by REaDLips Press

The RedWing Chronicles – Ron Terranova

Tourists in the Country of Love – Jo Rousseau

How to Throw a Psychic a Surprise Party – Noreen Lace

Upcoming Releases

Our Gentle Sins – Noreen Lace

Made in the USA
Monee, IL
30 September 2021